THE
LANGUAGE
OF
MARRIED LOVE

Preston and Genie Dyer

D1733413

CONVENTION PRESS

Nashville, Tennessee

5131-69

This book is the text for course 17109 in the subject area
The Christian Family in the Church Study Course.

Dewey Decimal Classification Number: 306.8
Subject Heading: MARRIAGE

Printed in the United States of America

Family Ministry Department
The Sunday School Board of the Southern Baptist Convention
127 Ninth Avenue North
Nashville, Tennessee 37234

ACKNOWLEDGEMENTS

Scripture quotations marked NIV are from the HOLY BIBLE
New International Version, copyright © 1978, New York
Bible Society. Used by permission.

Scripture quotations marked NASB are from the *New American
Standard Bible.* Copyright © The Lockman Foundation,
1960, 1962, 1963, 1968, 1971, 1972, 1973, 1975,
1977. Used by permission.

Unless otherwise indicated, Scripture quotations are
from the King James Version.

CONTENTS

MEET THE DYERS

Genie and Preston Dyer are marriage and family specialists. They have been on the staff at Baylor University in Waco, Texas, for the last eighteen years. Dr. Preston Dyer has over twenty years experience in the family field as therapist, educator, and researcher. The Dyers are active in the marriage and family enrichment movement. For over ten years they have concentrated much of their professional time and energy on helping married couples and families maximize the potential that exists in their close relationships. They have traveled widely leading marriage enrichment events, speaking at family life conferences, leading workshops and training other couples to lead enrichment activities. They have developed programs for engaged couples, a comprehensive marriage enrichment program for churches, and a family enrichment program for the parents of college freshmen. They are co-authors of a number of articles in the family field.

The Dyers are certified as leaders and as basic trainers by the Association for Couples in Marriage Enrichment and currently serve as president-couple of the Association. They have been married twenty-seven years and have a daughter and son.

INTRODUCTION

In 1974, we had been married fourteen years. Preston was preparing to return to graduate school. This meant he would be away from home during the week and return home for the weekend. Preston was consumed with worries about finances and his own ability to handle doctoral-level studies. We were both concerned about the drastic change in our life-style, especially spending time apart. Until then, we had not been separated for more than a few days at a time.

Had someone asked, we would have said immediately, "We have a good marriage." We were reared in Christian homes with parents who had loving marriages. We were active in our church as deacons and as co-teachers of a couples Sunday School class. But now, we were facing a major change in our lives. Genie particularly felt a concern for what might happen to our relationship over the coming two years. We had been around the university long enough to have seen a number of other people in the same situation. Too often, one partner earned an advanced degree, but in the process, the couple lost their marriage.

One evening we were sitting in Preston's study. He was feverishly trying to figure out how we could survive financially. Genie finally voiced the feelings that had been tugging at her for weeks. "I'm worried about what could happen to us," she said. Up to that point in our marriage, she had not spoken openly about feelings; our relationship had never been a topic of conversation. After all we had a "good marriage." Why talk about it? Perhaps it was the newness of Genie's openness, but for the first time, we faced the fact that divorce was something that could happen to us.

We communicated well about topical issues like finances, the children, and household tasks; but neither of us really knew how to talk about our relationship. Each of us knew what we wanted from the other, but not how to ask for it. We both needed more appreciation and affirmation from the other. We understood each other only superficially, having little knowledge of the other's deeper thoughts, feelings, and wants.

These represented disappointments for us, and certainly limited the intimacy we so much craved. But neither of us recognized these disappointments as potentially damaging to our relationship. There were many satisfying things about our marriage. We loved each other very much, and were in agreement on most of our goals and values. We enjoyed each other's company, and shared many joint interests. Even at that point, we were best friends. So while we were both aware of disappointments, we would have given our marriage an overall rating of okay.

The idea that marriage was something you had to work at was not a part of our preparation for marriage. We believed that if you were good, Christian people, you would just naturally have a good marriage. The corollary to that was that if things were not exactly as you wanted in your marriage, there really was not much you could do about it. For fourteen years, we had basically operated on that principle. We had simply allowed our marriage to develop on its own. Fortunately, in most areas, it had developed well.

Now we were faced with a new situation that challenged that assumption. Would the new stresses brought about by a different life-style exaggerate the disappointments we both felt? Would our marriage continue to grow in a healthy direction? Would it last? Having seen the failure of many marriages among our Christian friends, we knew the answer could be no.

Several years later, we heard Dr. David Mace, a pioneer in

marriage counseling and marriage enrichment, discussing the necessity of couples working together in their marriages. He described a marriage on the wedding day as being like a vacant lot on which building supplies—lumber, bricks, and roofing—have been stacked. All of the elements are there for building a house, but there is no house. On their wedding day, a couple has only the raw materials with which to build a marriage. If the marriage is to be a good one, the couple must be committed to work for the intentional growth of that marriage. It was that basic concept of marriage enrichment that we were struggling with in Preston's study that evening. "I want us to be together when you get your doctorate," Genie said. "What can we do?"

That was the beginning of marriage enrichment for us. It was at that point that we accepted, with God's help, the responsibility for consciously working for the development of our relationship. For the first time, we decided we did not want to leave our relationship to chance. We made a covenant with each other and God to work together for the growth of our relationship.

What we want to share with you in this book is our struggle over the last fourteen years to have a good marriage. We don't want to give the impression that we have a perfect marriage. Far from it. We have found, however, that by setting goals for growth and mutually committing ourselves to the growth of our marriage, we have experienced a new level of excitement and satisfaction. Most importantly, we now have confidence in our ability to direct our marriage in the way we want it to go. We have discovered that when we hit low spots, we know how to pull ourselves out of the doldrums. While we both continue to dislike conflict, we have learned to accept it and manage it as a creative force for growth. We no longer blame the other for a lack of intimacy; we individually work to create it.

This book is for couples who have good or at least okay

marriages. We are distressed not only by the number of divorces that occur annually, but also by the number of people who lack real fulfillment in marriage. A good guess is that only 10 percent of all marriages today are satisfying. It does not have to be that way. Couples can have exciting, supportive, and mutually fulfilling marriages. But, such marriages don't just happen. They are not the result of luck or even personal favors from a loving God. Christians may have a better chance of creating good marriages, but they are not immune to unhappy ones. Experiencing the love of God and knowing the Scripture help prepare for the task, but every couple must commit to work intentionally for growth if marriage is to be satisfying.

The process started for us when Genie changed a communication pattern. Marriage enrichment is much more than communication. Nevertheless, without effective communication it is impossible to work on other issues like conflict, sexuality, time management, spirituality, parenting, and intimacy. So our emphasis in this book is on improving communication. There is nothing magic or even hard about being a good communicator. It is a matter of learning some basic skills and principles and then practicing them as you would a golf or tennis technique. At first they may feel uncomfortable or artificial because they are new. Or, you may think each time you try one your partner will think, "Oh, I know what he's doing!" Don't give up. With time the skills will become a part of you. As you hear each other attempting the skills, accept that as a gift to you and your relationship. It means you are working to have a better marriage.

Most of these skills are described in Chapters 3 and 4. In Chapter 1 we explore God's purpose for marriage and the importance of communication in achieving that purpose. Chapter 2 deals with issues that affect communication. The last two chapters apply communication skills to two principal tasks in marriage. Chapter 5 deals with anger and conflict and Chapter 6 with intimacy and marital growth.

We have written the book with couples in mind. This does not mean that individuals will not find it helpful or cannot work on their marriage alone. It is, however, easier and more fun with a partner. For couples, we suggest that you set aside an hour and a half at a time to work with the book. Read the chapter together, stopping to discuss and apply ideas to your relationship. In each chapter you will find exercises to help apply the ideas presented. Please do not skip these. Stop and work through them as they occur in the chapter. Take plenty of time. Their primary purpose is to get you involved and talking about an issue or to give you an opportunity to practice a particular set of skills. It is very important that you do not get into an argument over them. We want working together to be a pleasant experience for you. If you feel yourself getting too defensive or perceive that your partner may be, suggest that you stop for a while. But, make an appointment to return to it later, being sure to set a specific time to try again.

Most of what is here we have learned from other people. We have drawn heavily on the wisdom of our teachers and others who have written and lectured on the subject. David and Vera Mace have been our mentors in marriage enrichment; and we have used much from his teaching on love, anger, and conflict. Sherrod Miller and his colleagues at Interpersonal Communications Programs, Inc., have greatly increased our own ability to communicate. Our understanding of marital interaction has been enhanced by the works of Richard Stuart and Carlfred Broderick who are outstanding marriage therapists. John Howell and Joyce and Clifford Penner stand out among the many who have influenced our understanding of God's purpose for marriage. For those we fail to acknowledge, we apologize.

Finally, we are indebted to the many couples with whom we have done enrichment and therapy through the years. As they have opened their marriages to us, we have learned and had our marriage enriched. This is particularly true of the five couples in our own marriage enrichment support group with whom we have met monthly for the last ten years. This group, the other marriage enrichment groups at Lake Shore Baptist Church, and couples in the U.S. and around the world with whom we have been involved through the Association for Couples in Marriage Enrichment, confirm our faith in the marriage enrichment process and the goodness of marriage.

We sincerely hope you find the chapters that follow helpful in enriching your marriage.

Chapter One

MARRIAGE
AND THE IMPORTANCE
OF COMMUNICATION

"GENIE AND PRESTON, what is unique about your marriage?" a young wife asked in the first marriage enrichment retreat we led. We were caught off guard since neither of us had ever considered that particular question. We looked at each other and after what seemed like several minutes Genie answered, "Perhaps it is that we are best friends. I would rather be with Preston than with anyone else. We each have other friends, but when it gets right down to it, I would rather spend my time with him. And I sense he feels the same way." Preston squeezed Genie's hand and nodded his agreement to the group. Later in the evening we had the chance to discuss this in private and agreed that for us, close companionship is the principal purpose of our marriage. Our study of both biblical material and contemporary social science has confirmed this conclusion.

THE PURPOSE OF MARRIAGE

Family texts over the years have provided long lists of the functions of the family. As society has changed, so have these lists. Most modern texts list only two functions of the family: (1) providing emotional support to each other, and (2) having and rearing children. While the second of these has always been on the list, the first began appearing in the 1960s. A generation ago only a few couples would have identified companionship as a key purpose of marriage. Few young couples today would see anything unique about the answer Genie gave. The concept of being married to one's best friend is rapidly becoming the expected norm.

When Preston started teaching family courses in the mid-sixties, the most frequent response from women to the question of what they wanted from marriage was first, children, and second, financial security. To the same question men most often answered sex and children. The current generation of students answers that question almost universally: companionship, friendship, and emotional support. Many young men and women express it exactly as Genie did, "I want a marriage partner with whom I can be best friends."

Exercise A: Marital Expectations

1. Read Genesis 1 and 2.
2. How do you interpret God's purpose for marriage?
3. What do you want from your marriage?
4. Share your responses to the above questions with your partner.

God's Purpose for Marriage

The Genesis account provides an extraordinary view of God's purpose for marriage. God created man and placed him in the garden. The garden provided an environment in which all of Adam's physical needs were met. He was given authority over all the other creatures which shared the garden with him. God paraded before him a whole menagerie of animal life; yet Adam was not able to settle a strange longing. In the garden with all of the animals, Adam was still lonely for one of his own kind. He searched through the whole animal kingdom to find a way to overcome his loneliness, but there was no remedy. Out of His love for Adam, God exclaimed, "It is not good for the man to be alone; I will make him a helper suitable for him" (Gen. 2:18, NASB).

God had given Adam authority over the animals, but authority can provide a barrier for relationships. So God, not wanting to see Adam lonely, created for him one of his own kind; but one not exactly like him. Not a clone, because he would soon become bored with one who was his mirror image. But one who, like Adam himself, was created in the image and glory of God. One who was similar enough to be a companion but different enough to make life exciting. When God introduced this new creation to Adam, his eyes lit up, his heart pounded and he shouted with joy, "This is now bone of my bones, and flesh of my flesh" (Gen. 2:23, NASB). For in this creature Adam found a partner with whom he could share every dimension of his life.

Adam's glad acceptance of the new partner and his joyous response provide us with an exhilarating description of his recognition of their oneness. She was his ideal partner and they were suited for each other in every way. Not only was she radiant in her loveliness, she also had intelligence to match his. Above all else, she, too, was created in the image of God. Eve was for Adam, as he was for her, God's solution to loneliness.

God's creation of man was in accordance with a particular design, and that design was the image of God. In Genesis 1:26-27, God said, "Let Us make man in Our image according to Our likeness . . . And God created man in His own image, in the image of God He created him; male and female. He created them" (NASB). Adam and Eve were both made in God's image. Maleness and femaleness are representative of God's image.

What does it mean to be created in God's image? It means that we are created to be in relationship. It means we have the capacity to experience a relationship with God which the animals do not have. But it also means we have the capacity to have relationship with each other.

An understanding of the human side of this relationship grows out of the concept of oneness. The biblical reference to Adam and Eve becoming one flesh certainly refers to and celebrates the sexual side of their relationship; but, being in the image of God includes a higher level of functioning than just animalistic sexuality. In the animal world, union is based on the function of hormones and requires only a rapid, physical, sexual release. Oneness in human relationship includes the total expression of ourselves physically, spiritually, and emotionally.

Not many examples of that kind of relationship are found in the Old Testament. In spite of the beauty and potential of the first union, marriage is seen most often in the Old Testament as something akin to a business deal. Love was not commanded and it was not even expected. The primary functions of marriage were utilitarian, and they have remained so throughout most of human history.

With the coming of Christ, God's original plan for marriage was reasserted. The New Testament introduced the concept of love between a husband and wife as an expected part of the marriage relationship. The husband-wife relationship was to be built on the same kind of love Christ lavished on the church. "Husbands, love your wives, just as Christ loved the church and gave Himself up for her . . . In this same way, husbands ought to love their wives as their own bodies. He who loves his wife loves himself" (Eph. 2:25,28, NIV). Love became the guiding principle for how married partners were to behave in relation to each other.

This concept was so contrary to the thinking of men and women in New Testament times that for the most part it fell on deaf ears. Marriage based on love and emotional fulfillment in a spousal relationship was just not a part of their culture. As we have seen, however, it was a part of God's original plan. With the coming of Christ, that plan was brought into focus and recognized as one of God's good gifts to His people.

Covenant: God's Plan for Marriage
In both the Old and New Testaments, God's plan for marriage is most often described in terms of covenant. This refers to a mutual agreement or commitment entered into by two or more parties. It is the concept used in the Bible to describe God's relationship to the "new Israel"—the church (Gen. 9,15; Ex. 19; Hos. 2; 2 Cor. 3:6; Heb. 7:2, 8:6, 13:24). Covenant carries with it some of the ideas of contract. The word contract, in a contemporary sense, often suggests a tit-for-tat agreement in which the parties pledge to exchange one specific behavior for one equally specific action. When this sense of contract is applied to marriage, it suggests rigidity, legalism, and coldness.

The biblical concept of covenant suggests a flexible, dynamic process which is more personal than legalistic. It is one which gives partners options and includes a commitment to continue the contract even when one or the other fails in some part. The covenant relationship described in the Bible suggests six dimensions of God's plan for marriage: commitment, partnership, communication, intimacy, reconciliation, and steadfast love. These six dimensions offer the means by which we can achieve God's purpose for marriage.

Mutual commitment is the foundation of the relationship between the two partners in a covenant marriage. It reflects a commitment to the lordship of Jesus Christ in each of their individual lives and in their marital relationship, and a commitment to strive together for the intentional growth of their relationship and to a life of shared ministry.

Mutual commitment creates for the marital pair a *partnership* that has purpose. Covenant marriage acknowledges the sacredness and uniqueness of each human personality. It is this very uniqueness that, in part, attracts each to the other. They are persons long before they are partners, and nothing in the marriage relationship diminishes the personhood of either partner.

Because each member of the partnership is a unique individual, a *communication* process that leads to the understanding of each other is an absolute essential in the covenant marriage. It is through communication that our physical, spiritual, and emotional oneness is experienced. It is the means by which we bridge our separateness.

Intimacy develops out of understanding. In a covenant relationship, commitment, partnership, and communication make intimacy possible. Intimacy refers to a sense of closeness and openness to each and requires the sharing of total personhood. For most couples it is the desire for a sense of togetherness in a truly trusting, open relationship that draws them to marriage. This is very close to the biblical concept of oneness.

Reconciliation is the fifth characteristic of the covenant marriage. As much as we may desire intimacy, it will not always be there. Because we are human, we will sometimes fail to live up to our commitments. Regardless of the level of our skill, communication will sometimes break down. As a result, the closeness of our relationship will be threatened. It simply is not true that couples who have good marriages don't experience bad times. What is more likely is couples

with good marriages know how to move out of those bad times through a process of reconciliation and renewal.

The final dimension of the covenant relationship is *steadfast love.* This is the kind of love described in the New Testament as *agapé.* In modern terminology it is "unconditional love." Whatever it is called, it is love without any qualifications that leads the couple into mutual commitment with each other. It is steadfast love that undergirds the partnership and motivates the partners to struggle with communication until understanding actually takes place. It is steadfast love that keeps them together even when the intimacy is not there. It is steadfast love that drives them toward reconciliation. As Christians we experience Christ's unconditional love over and over again.

Is the desire for a permanent marriage based on close companionship an impossible dream? We think not. The six dimensions of covenant marriage point the way to achieving just such a relationship in a time when it is not only desired but desperately needed.

Emergence of Companionship Marriage

Over the last seventy-five years, changes in our culture have encouraged the development of a model of marriage based on companionship. In the past, men sought other men as best friends and women sought other women as best friends. The gap in men's and women's roles almost made this essential. Other than children, husbands and wives had little to talk about. Increasingly, the rigid distinction between men's and women's roles has become more flexible and provided a bridge between the worlds of the two genders. As women have taken their place beside men in school, the workplace, and the political arena, they have shared more experiences on which to build a relationship based on friendship.

Couples marrying in the late 1980s have far different expectations of marriage than did their grandparents, or even their parents. Fifty years ago a wife had little choice but to look to her husband for financial security while depending on mother, sisters, and female friends for emotional support. Today, most women are far more confident of their ability to provide for their own financial needs. Yet they find themselves living in an increasingly lonely environment, often isolated from former sources of emotional support. Contemporary husbands, on the other hand, are less likely than their fathers or grandfathers to define themselves solely in terms of work or to look at their jobs as their sole source of fulfillment. No longer expected to hide his feelings and emotional needs, he too seeks shelter from the loneliness of a competitive world. Both expect a marriage relationship that fulfills their needs for friendship, acceptance, and intimacy.

Like Adam in the Genesis account, many people in today's world find themselves with an abundance of opportunities for individual fulfillment in an overly stimulating environment, yet still find themselves lonely. To find the solution to loneliness, contemporary couples are looking for a different kind of marriage—not one like their grandparents or, for most, even like their parents, or like those typical of the New or Old Testament. They are looking for a marriage based on companionship, one strangely similar to that described in the early chapters of Genesis.

Without question, today's companionship marriage has its problems. Our high divorce rate attests to that. In spite of those problems, we believe that today's emphasis on the significance of relationship and mutual support is closer to God's original plan for marriage than was the older model. We are convinced God's original purpose in marriage was to satisfy the human need for emotional intimacy through close companionship. "For this cause a man shall leave his father and his mother, and shall cleave to his wife" (Gen. 2:24, NASB). Today, in a secular, depersonalized world, we need that kind of companionship, perhaps as never before.

Christians and non-Christians alike have been frustrated in their attempt to establish a companionship-based marriage. A relationship-oriented marriage requires skills that most of us have not acquired naturally. These are primarily human relationship skills. At a minimum, partners in a companionship marriage must have skills that enable them to: (1) understand each other; (2) deal with conflict and negotiate their differences; and (3) build oneness through spiritual, physical, and emotional intimacy. Effective communication is a tool that underpins each of these and, therefore, an essential for partners seeking a companionship marriage.

THE IMPORTANCE OF COMMUNICATION

Effective communication is only one of the six dimensions of covenant marriage. In and of itself, it will not produce a successful marriage. Yet, clear communication is essential to the other five dimensions. We use communication to handle disagreements, to make decisions, and to set rules. It plays an important part in drawing partners closer or pushing them apart. To be able to live together satisfactorily, two people must be able to make their wishes known, to understand the requests made by the other, and to establish shared goals.

It is impossible not to communicate. The very absence of overt communication is communication. If Preston comes into the house and goes straight to his study without speaking to Genie, he has communicated. Communication involves what we say, the way we say it, how we listen when someone else is speaking, and our nonverbal behavior. Communication is the sharing of our perceptions of the world about us—what we think; our feelings or emotions; and our expectations, wants, and needs. Through communication we satisfy our need to connect to others, to influence and be influenced by others, to give affirmation and be affirmed, and to give and receive affection. Communication is the meeting of meaning. When the message inside of you meets the message inside your partner across the bridge of words, tones, acts, and deeds; then understanding occurs—then you know you have communicated effectively.

Exercise B: What Do We Talk About?

1. List three topics about which you and your partner communicate well.

2. Now, list three topics that you talk about but often do not feel understood after you have talked.
3. Finally, list any meaningful topics that you do NOT talk about. Perhaps you have tried to discuss these in the past, and conflict arose so you now avoid them.
4. When you have finished, share your list with your partner. How close were you in your assessments of your communication patterns? Which of the topics on the second list would you like to work on to improve your understanding of each other? Are there any topics on the third list that you would like to open for discussion? If so, we believe some of the skills discussed in Chapters 3 and 4 will help to do that.

The Biblical Model for Communication

God created human beings to communicate with Him and with each other. The part of the brain that gives us the ability to speak and to understand language is larger in human beings than in any other living creature. Language allows us to convey information, ask questions, share emotions, and give thanks.

While communication is important in every marriage, it takes on special significance in the marriage of Christians. When Christians marry, a partnership is created including the man, the woman, and God. God's understanding is complete; but the human partners must work to communicate to each other their thoughts, feelings, and desires if there is to be understanding. Understanding increases the stability and strength of the partnership and helps the couple to maintain their commitments to each other and to God. Even as God has revealed Himself to us, we must be willing to reveal ourselves to each other.

Revelation is the biblical model for communication. The Bible itself is, in fact, the record of God's revelation of Himself to persons. God has made and continues to make

Himself known to us in a variety of ways. God's ultimate communication, however, came in the form of His Son, Jesus. "In these last days [God] has spoken to us in His Son . . . and He is the . . . exact representation of His nature" (Heb. 1:2-3, NASB). God disclosed Himself through Jesus. John acknowledged: "In the beginning was the Word, and the Word was with God, and the Word was God . . . And the Word became flesh, and dwelt among us, and we beheld His glory, glory as of the only begotten from the Father . . . No man has seen God at any time; He has explained Him" (John 1:1,14,18, NASB). God's purpose throughout history has been to draw His people closer to Him. His purpose in revealing Himself to us through the prophets of old, through Jesus, and through the Holy Spirit is that we might understand Him more clearly and draw more intimately into relationship with Him. Communication has that same purpose—to promote the kind of understanding that leads to companionship and intimacy—in all human relationships, but particularly in the marital relationship.

Marital Happiness and Communication

Several years ago a newspaper article reported that the average couple married ten years or more, spends only thirty-seven minutes a week in significant communication. Some who have studied the American family for years take an even more pessimistic view. They argue that meaningful communication is virtually nonexistent by middle age. Husbands and wives become so accustomed to one another that they seldom talk at all.

Professionals have studied extensively the relationship between communication and marital satisfaction. These studies show marriages tend to be extremely happy when both partners are good communicators. They indicate satisfaction with the marriage rises and falls with the level of communication.

What do couples with good marriages talk about? They talk about themselves—their hopes; problems; self-doubt; and feelings of joy, anger, or excitement. And, they discuss their relationship, openly sharing positive feelings about their life together as well as bothersome aspects of the marriage. They also communicate affection and understanding and use communication as a problem-solving tool in resolving disagreements and making decisions.

Just as effective communication appears to be a basic ingredient of a successful marriage, faulty communication is a major cause of failure. Marriage and family therapists consistently report communication as the number one problem of couples seeking their help.

So the evidence strongly suggests that effective communication is an essential ingredient for a happy marriage. The great tragedy of so many marriages today is not the threat of divorce, adultery, or abuse, but of boredom and complacency. Because they do not know how to communicate effectively or because they choose not to, too many couples are willing to accept a mediocre relationship—a relationship in which neither really knows the other, and neither is willing to take the risk of openly sharing thoughts, feelings, and desires with the other. As a result, neither partner feels understood or appreciated. Some of these marriages exist for years, taking their toll from both partners. Others last only as long as neither partner finds greater hope for fulfillment outside the marriage.

The Complexity of Communication
As essential as effective communication is, it is also complex. Communication is complex partly because it occurs at several levels. As we said earlier, it is impossible not to communicate. Everything we do or say transmits information to our partners. At one level we simply exchange information through words. But at another level we make an indirect

statement about our relationship. For example, the husband who belittles his wife's ideas and discounts her feelings is sending two messages: the overt message about those specific ideas and feelings, and an indirect message that she and her thoughts and feelings have little worth to him.

Every message contains an indirect comment about whether the person addressed is liked or disliked. At one level this may be expressed verbally; at another, nonverbally. As a general principle, positive evaluations can be expressed either verbally or nonverbally; but negative evaluations should always be expressed in words as a request for change.

If there is conflict between the two, the nonverbal is more likely to be received. In intimate relationships effective communication depends almost entirely on the attitudes of the two people involved. If Genie is anxious, fearful, or angry when she tries to communicate with Preston, those identical feelings are likely to be aroused in him. On the other hand, if she radiates satisfaction, love, excitement, or joy, he is likely to send those emotions back to her. Consequently, your interaction will greatly improve if you try to make the most positive possible interpretations of your partner's messages. Couples who constantly search out each other's negative messages have a high level of unhappiness.

Clear communication, then, is far more than an exchange of words. It affects and is affected by our relationship. It is both self-expression and listening. It is words and behavior. It is impossible not to communicate.

Open Communication: Help or Hindrance?
Perhaps at this point you are wondering what kind of communication we are talking about. Some practitioners in the field believe "open communication" is synonymous with a happy marriage. By "open communication" they mean expressing every last one of your personal thoughts and feelings

to your partner. At one point in time we tried to practice this type of communication. Our own experience convinced us that unbridled communication is not helpful to a marriage and may very well harm the relationship.

Many of us bought into the idea of totally open communication simply because we were aware of the results of not revealing enough to our partners. But simply jumping from one extreme to another is not the answer. Brutally frank communication is a threat to any relationship. A husband's unchecked and untimely expression of negative feelings without a balance of positive comments and affirmation may seriously damage his wife's self-esteem. Or, a wife's frequent expression of dissatisfaction and criticism may undermine her husband's confidence in himself and in the marriage. As we have worked with couples over the years, we have become all too aware of the fact that words once spoken cannot be taken back. A spouse may never forget some of the painful things said by a partner.

If unbridled, total self-disclosure is not the objective of communication, what is? Richard Stuart, the marriage therapist of whom we spoke earlier, has suggested the principle of "measured honesty." What we say must be the truth, but it also must pass the test of concern for our partner and concern for the relationship. Stuart suggests monitoring communication to express mostly positive reactions and only a few important, timely requests for change. To practice the principle of measured honesty, try asking yourself these questions before you speak: Is it true? Is it positive? And, if not, is it really worth the risk? We will talk more about how to give both positive and negative feedback in Chapter 4.

GOALS OF COMMUNICATION

What do you hope to gain for yourself and your marriage by learning to communicate more effectively? The goals for general communication differ somewhat from those of marital communication. Often, in general communication a major goal is to be so eloquent and persuasive that you are able to get whatever you wish from your listeners. Relationship may not be of great concern. On the contrary, in communicating with a marital partner, care for the partner and the relationship are the key objectives. We would like for you to pause here to think about your own personal communication goals using the following exercise.

Exercise C: Identifying Communication Goals

1. Here is a list of possible communication goals. Each of you go through and mark three to five you would particularly like to accomplish. Don't look at your partner's list. You may want to add some we missed.

GOALS
a. Develop more ways to talk
b. Find more to talk about
c. Understand myself better
d. Understand my partner better
e. Feel heard and understood
f. Avoid disagreements
g. Increase self-worth
h. Deescalate hostility and fights
i. Find new and better ways of handling day-to-day situations
j. Feel closer, more intimate

    k. Be more persuasive in my arguments
    l. Express more affection and appreciation

2. When you both have identified your goals, share them, discussing the reasons for your choices.

3. You and your partner may have very different goals. That's okay. It just confirms that you are two different people. You can work on the process of communication together while working toward different goals.

4. As you start each new chapter, review your goals and think about how that chapter might help you achieve them. As you see your partner working on his/her goals, be sure to acknowledge the effort.

We would like to suggest three specific goals essential to the companionship type of marriage discussed in this chapter: increased understanding of each other, increased ability to negotiate disagreements, and increased ability to build your own and your partner's self-esteem. Are these three on your list?

Better Understanding
A marriage can tolerate far more disagreement than it can misunderstanding. By understanding we mean having a good sense of what our partner is thinking, feeling, and wanting. Many people believe this just happens automatically in marriage. It does not! Preston can begin to understand Genie only when she tells him what is happening inside of her. One of the greatest myths of marriage is that husbands and wives can somehow crawl inside the other's skin and know what they think, or feel, or want. I can begin to understand you only as you are willing to reveal yourself to me.

Charles and Jackie had been married for six years when they came to us for counseling. It was Jackie's second marriage and her teenage son, John, lived with them. They both genuinely loved the boy, but they had sharp disagreements about parenting styles. Charles saw Jackie's permissiveness as resulting in serious problems; Jackie saw his more rigid style as harsh.

In one session, Charles confronted Jackie with her inconsistency in parenting. When John turned sixteen, he had wanted to purchase a car of his own. Charles did not think this was a good idea. John's school grades were already only average, and he would have to get a part-time job to pay for the car. Finally, an agreement was reached. John would be allowed to buy a car; but to keep the car, he would have to maintain at least his current grade average. If his grades dropped, he would have to sell the car. All three had agreed to this. Charles helped John select a used car, and together they put it in top-notch condition.

The following semester, as Charles had feared, John's grades dropped severely. Charles reminded him of the agreement and insisted he sell the car. John resisted and Jackie refused to enforce the agreement. Charles was completely frustrated. He felt powerless and was angry with John and Jackie.

As we listened to Charles talk, it was hard not to agree with his reasoning. Jackie tried to justify her position but could not counter his logic. As she began to cry softly, we encouraged her to tell Charles what she was feeling. Finally, she said, "John is the only one of my three children who chose to live with me. The other two live with their dad. He gave each of them a car. We couldn't afford to give John a car. I feel so guilty because he had to buy his own. I know it's inconsistent, but I just can't take it away from him. I'm afraid he might leave me to live with his dad." As Charles listened to her and heard her feelings, he began to understand in a way that superseded all of his logic. He pulled her into his big arms and against his chest. She sobbed quietly, and he said, "I see now; I understand." Charles and Jackie still had issues to work out, but what they learned was that the ability to understand each other was far more important than agreement.

We should warn you that as you begin to communicate more effectively, you may actually find yourselves disagreeing more. As you understand each other better, you may become more aware of your differences and strongly disagree. Remember, because you are unique creations, you are bound to differ in many ways.

Negotiation
Effective communication provides an efficient means for negotiating disagreements. When negotiating, partners state directly what they want and why, rather than trying to get it through indirect means. They then work through their differences in a straightforward fashion. This process produces the added benefit of increased understanding and affirmation. Often in dealing with our partners, we forfeit the opportunity for better understanding because we choose to manipulate rather than negotiate.

While the overt decision to ask directly may appear to be selfish, it is in fact much less selfish than the covert decision to manipulate. Manipulation can take many forms. It is any subtle or indirect action one takes to ensure getting what s/he wants. Manipulation does not lead to understanding or affirmation. Many times it causes anger, hurt, or bitterness because the manipulated partner feels used or just plain dumb. The manipulator does not feel affirmed because what s/he got was not freely and lovingly given. Even though I may get what I want through manipulation, if I cause you pain or miss a chance for affirmation, I still lose relationship.

Both manipulation and ignoring differences lead to an "I lose/you lose" situation, while successful negotiation results in "I win/you win." In good marriages, partners strive for conditions where both win and, in so doing, build self-esteem and esteem for their relationship.

Building Self, Partner, and Relationship Esteem

The very best skills alone are not enough unless couples approach communication with the desire to communicate with each other in ways that build positive feelings about themselves, their partner, and their relationship. In one of our first couples' communication courses, a very bright, young theology student participated. He picked up the skills very quickly. When we asked for volunteers to demonstrate the skills for the class, he was always eager to volunteer. By the second or third time he volunteered, we realized that, while using the skills correctly from a technical standpoint, he was in fact using them to tear his partner down. The more skillful he became, the more damage he did to her self-esteem.

Dr. Nick Stinett, Dean of the College of Education and Psychology at Pepperdine University, has for many years studied the strengths of healthy families. One of the traits he has consistently found is that in strong families, members like themselves and each other. Moreover, they affirm each other often. That is, they communicate through words and behavior their appreciation of each other and their family. If a couple accepts affirmation as a communication goal, then each partner works toward building each other's self-esteem and their mutual esteem for the relationship.

Look again at the goals you have selected. Talk with your partner and see if together you want to make any changes. In the chapters that follow, we will be focusing on specific ideas to help you achieve your goals. Remember, if you really want to improve the quality of your marriage, the best way to start is by improving your communication.

Chapter Two

BARRIERS AND BRIDGES

VIRGINIA SATIR, the famous family therapist and communications specialist, once said that the primary purpose of communication is to bridge the gap of our separateness—to move us from separateness to togetherness. No matter how much we may wish it, another person cannot crawl inside our skin to know us. If I want my partner to understand me, I must somehow bridge the gap between our separate selves. To accomplish that, I must be able to communicate the message inside me to my partner in a way that he or she gains a better understanding of what is happening within me. Communication then becomes the bridge that helps create our togetherness.

Unfortunately, married couples often end up building walls or barriers between themselves rather than bridges. Sometimes we do this accidentally, but at other times we do it purposefully. As much as we want to be understood, the risk of letting another person really know us often creates a fear that is stronger than our need to be known.

In this chapter we want to look at some barriers couples frequently erect that block their togetherness. We have discovered that often, when couples become aware of the barriers they construct, they can tear them down and create bridges. Some barriers are fairly universal; that is, almost all couples have to contend with them at some time during their marriages. Others are distinctive to the individual couple. We would like for you to try the following exercise as a means of identifying both the barriers and the bridges to communication in your marriage.

Exercise D: Identifying Bridges and Barriers

1. Each of you will need a sheet of paper. Draw a line down the middle of the page. Head the first column "Bridges" and the second "Barriers." Now take about five minutes to list on the left side those things which you think build bridges between you and your partner—that is, those things that increase your ability to communicate with each other in a way that moves you from separateness to togetherness. When Genie did this exercise, the first item she listed under "Bridges" was "spending time together."

2. Now on the right side list those things that you believe block your communication with each other—those behaviors or circumstances which wall off your separateness. Preston started this list with "anger."

3. When you have finished, take turns sharing your lists of "bridges." Celebrate together those things which enrich your communication.

4. Now discuss your perceived barriers with one another. Try not to blame or be defensive. Accept each other's list as an assessment of where you are in your communication.

You probably listed a number of barriers that we will not discuss in this chapter. Some of them we may address in other chapters. Others we hope you will be able to work on together as your communication skills increase. In this chapter we want to discuss three barriers that seem to cause problems for a great many couples: time, differences, and defensiveness. Did any of these appear on either of your lists?

TIME

Failure to set aside adequate time to be together may be the biggest barrier to communication most contemporary couples face. Communication, knowing and being known, demands, perhaps above all else, sufficient time for it to take place. Quality time or efficiently using the time available is important; but first and foremost, there must be time. God has been in the process of revealing Himself to us since the days of creation. Surely, we should expect it to take a lifetime to come to know and understand each other in a marriage. We know if we are to receive God's revelation of Himself to us, we must set aside special time for Bible study and prayer; but we often fail to accept the fact that we need special time every day to learn about our marital partner. That cannot be done if we are in perpetual motion, rushing from one activity to another, and totally out of energy by the time we have a few minutes together.

People in the United States have become addicted to having something to do all the time. Our schedules are full from daylight to bedtime. Our pace is frantic, and fatigue is a way of life. We act as though relationships grow by themselves. The simple fact is that, like other living things, relationships take time and nurturing. Although working on communication skills, as you are now doing with this book, can increase efficiency, quality communication still takes time. If you are not willing to take time to communicate, better skills alone will not be very helpful. Husbands and wives must have time on a regular basis to share their thoughts and feelings in a meaningful way.

Time becomes a bridge to communication when couples make sure there is adequate time and energy available to share feelings and discuss their relationship. When couples are courting and during the early years of marriage, they make sure they have time together. And much of that time together is spent discussing their relationship. However, after an intimate relationship is well established, partners tend to communicate less about their feelings and focus more on the functional aspects of their lives: schedules, bills, the children, and so on. These issues obviously need discussion, but not to the exclusion of discussions about each other's thoughts, feelings, and wants. When partners fail to discuss issues that are central to their relationship, they are less satisfied with their communication and their marriage.

Whereas before marriage a couple has to make arrangements to see each other, after marriage contact is a part of their daily routine. They no longer have to plan to be with the other. Since they have so much time together, it does not seem as necessary to plan time to communicate about their emotions, their goals, and what they want from the relationship. Many even forget the importance of frequently telling and showing how much they love, respect, and appreciate each other. Yet, as we pointed out in the first chapter, the quality of communication in the marriage depends on the exchange of personal information.

Couples who value quality communication give it a high priority in their time schedules. They arrange for time alone away from the television, the children, and other distractions so they can talk not only about the functional matters but also about themselves and their relationship.

Managing What We Do with Our Time

When we stress the importance of time together in our marriage enrichment events, we often see the participants' expressions register disbelief and total frustration. "You have got to be kidding! How can that be done with the kinds of lives we lead?" We do not want to be naive at this point. We are painfully aware of the pressures of time. We know what it is like to be a dual-career couple, and we remember vividly the problems of keeping up with our own schedules in addition to those of our children. No wonder time management is such an important workshop topic these days!

We have always looked on time management as a means of getting more activity into the time available. Recently, a friend proposed a new perspective that has changed our thinking. Time management, he suggests, is a means of getting rid of those things in your life which give you the least satisfaction to make more room to enjoy those things which give you the greatest satisfaction. To apply this to our own lives we did the following exercise. We would like for you to try it.

Exercise E: Priorities vs. Demands

1. Look over the following list of activities that require time and attention. Perhaps there are others in your life which need to be added. If so, add them to this list before you begin to work with it.

   > Money (achieving a higher living standard)
   > Financial security (keeping what you have)
   > Disciplines of faith (prayer, Bible study, etc.)
   > Spouse
   > Children
   > Church activities
   > House (cleaning, upkeep, beautifying)
   > Friends
   > Education (learning, not just pursuit of degrees)

Extended family
Job
Community service
Hobbies
Leisure

2. Now, each of you separately list on a sheet of paper the items in order of priority as you see them at this time. The item you believe should have the top priority will be at the top of your list, and the one you think should have the least priority will be on the bottom.
3. When you have assigned priorities, share your lists with each other. How close are you in your priorities? Discuss together how you arrived at your listings.
4. We are not through yet! Next, each of you look again at your list. This time arrange the issues from top to bottom based on the amount of time you spend on that issue. How different are the two lists you made? Do your current habits of spending time reflect your priorities? Share your list again and discuss your level of satisfaction with the way you spend your time. Are you both satisfied? If not, discuss specific activities which might be diminished to allow more time for the top priorities. Also discuss specific activities which might be added or magnified to reflect the top priorities.

When we did this exercise, we found a lot of differences in our priorities and the way we arranged our time. We have come to realize that if we want to live our lives by our priorities rather than by the demands others put on us, we have to be intentional about scheduling our time, particularly our time together.

Solving the Time Problem

Most people live by an appointment calendar, at least in their work. In fact, we have found that most people carry in their pockets or purses some kind of calendar. Using your calendar to arrange coupletime may be a technique you have overlooked.

Appointments are generally valued in the world of work. We suggest that at least once a week (Sunday night after church is a good time for many couples) you sit down together with your calendars. Look over your schedules for the next week keeping in mind your priorities. Identify some times that you can spend together and write those in your appointment book or calendar. Remember in selecting times that good communication and relationship building require energy.

Making appointments will not help much if you do not give the appointments with your spouse the same degree of importance and respect you give to others. We have learned that when someone calls to ask one of us to do something, it will not work to say, "Oh, I'm sorry I have plans to spend that evening with my wife." A typical response was, "With your wife! I have four other deacons who can meet at that time. You can be with her any time." What we do now is just say, "Gee, I'm sorry. I already have an appointment for that time." Since appointments are generally respected, the usual response is, "Okay! Let's look for another time."

How much time is enough time? That is a hard question, but one that deserves consideration. We believe that every couple needs to spend a minimum of twenty to thirty minutes together every day just to check in and let one another know where they are in their lives. We call this our "weather report time." David and Vera Mace, pioneers in the marriage enrichment movement, taught us an excellent exercise for getting started and making the most of this time. It is called the "Ten and Ten" exercise.

Exercise F: Ten and Ten

1. First, take ten minutes to get in touch with your feelings: emotions like excitement, anxiety, frustration, pride; or even physical feelings like a headache or being too full from eating. List these on a sheet of paper.

2. Now, share your lists with each other. One of you give one or two feelings from your list with some commentary about where the feeling comes from, and then the other do the same.
3. Continue until both have exhausted their lists. If you hit something controversial, don't try to settle it now. Make an appointment to work on it at a later time. This should be a pleasant time for you. Simply accept your partner's feelings as where he or she is right now. Feelings are not right or wrong. They are just feelings, and sharing them is a means of helping my partner know where I am. Our friends the Maces say they could no more start their day without their sharing time than they could without their devotional time.

Beyond the "daily weather report," couples also need a minimum of two hours a week to work hard on their relationships—to communicate both their celebrations and concerns about their shared lives. This is a time each needs to strive to hear the other's thoughts and feelings and to understand their meaning to that person. This can be a pleasant time even though you may deal with some difficult issues.

We enjoy going out for breakfast, so we often use our Saturday morning breakfast outing for this purpose. Lila and Stan find that they are less likely to get defensive if they talk in a quiet but public setting; so they have dinner together, often in a quiet, romantic restaurant.

Phillip, a physician, and Sheryl, who owns her own business, enjoy the few hours they have together at home. When they planned their new home they designed a "dialogue corner." It is no more than a pleasant little nook with two comfortable chairs arranged so they can look at each other. Perhaps most important, they have taught their two children to respect their privacy when they retreat there. This not only assures them the privacy they need, but also teaches the children the importance of communication between husbands and wives.

Couples also need some time each week for relaxation and entertainment to keep the marriage from being overcome by routine demands. This should be a time when concerns and conflicts are laid aside so both can concentrate on enjoying each other's company. This will be easier to do if the daily sharing time is allotted and used well. Even if everything is not settled, both have the assurance that there will be another time to work on the leftover concerns.

Planning "dates" is an excellent way to incorporate relaxation and entertainment into your schedule. Tom and Marge set aside at least one night each weekend for a date. Sometimes they go out alone; sometimes they invite friends to join them. At other times they invite friends in for the evening; and at times they choose to stay at home together to talk, to share a television program or tape, or to read aloud.

Should you decide to date, be careful to see that you share responsibility for planning and child care. If this task always falls on the shoulders of one person, the date may become more of a chore than a reviving experience. Also, if you need suggestions on couple activities that will enrich your relationship, *Home Life* magazine contains a monthly feature entitled "Coupletime."

The times we mention here are a minimum. Many couples will want much more. Others, because of life-styles, will not be able to arrange time as we have suggested and will have to use their creativity to accomplish the same ends. Carol is a graduate student and Charles works a swing shift at the glass plant. They often go seven or eight days hardly seeing each other, much less having two hours to talk together. They maximize their time together as best they can on a daily and weekly basis, but there is just no time for extended conversation. To compensate for the time they lose, they have devised a plan for combining their serious dialogue time with relaxation and entertainment. Once every four to six weeks they plan a minivacation. Another couple swaps child care with them so they can take a Friday-night-and-all-day-Saturday, out-of-town trip. They find staying in a hotel and eating out taxes their budget, but probably no more than a weekly date. Devising ways to spend quality time together may take creativity, but it may be the best gift you can give yourself, your partner, and your relationship.

One last word about time. Time together does not guarantee good communication between a husband and wife. Some spouses have many hours together and do nothing but argue meaninglessly. Others share an almost wordless and boring routine of sameness. For communication in marriage to take place, we must speak words which truly share our thoughts, feelings, and inner lives. We are going to work on developing those very skills in the next chapter.

DIFFERENT COMMUNICATION STYLES

Sue often complains that her husband, Ted, does not talk to her enough. Ted, like many husbands, counters that Sue talks too much about trivial or uninteresting things. Sue stopped by Ted's office the other day and discovered that his secretary knew she had prepared his favorite dessert for him the night before and that he had loved it. On the same visit a co-worker mentioned to her that Ted had bragged to him about their daughter having made the tennis team at her school. "Why didn't you tell me how much you liked my dessert?" she asked Ted with frustration in her voice.

He became defensive and replied, "Well, after all, I ate two bowls didn't I?"

"Why didn't you tell Janie how proud you were of her for making the team?" she asked again with irritation.

Ted got flustered, shrugged his shoulders and said, "Oh, she knows."

Does Style Depend on Gender?
Researchers have just begun to study how much difference actually exists in the typical communication pattern of males and females. It appears that traditional sex-role learning does have some effect on how couples communicate. Sex-role socialization is the process of learning how to act in ways recognized as appropriate for one's sex. It is the development of behaviors that one considers to be masculine or feminine. Many men in our society, for example, are taught that expressing any emotion other than anger is unmasculine. Their model of masculinity may be someone like John Wayne or Clint Eastwood who, at least on the screen, seems to have difficulty expressing tenderness or affection. John Wayne's strong, silent type has certainly been a stereotype of the traditional masculine image in the United States for a long time.

Silence can be a sign of respect and commitment to hear what a partner has to say without interrupting; but in some situations, silence conveys something other than a willingness to listen. The sender may interpret the silence as rejection, as a refusal to become vulnerable through self-disclosure, or as a decision the conversation is not worthwhile. Research has suggested that one of these interpretations is much more likely to be made by a female when the silent listener is a male.

In contrast to males, women have been taught that the expression of positive emotion, such as love, is important and necessary in close relations. To become angry and shout is considered to be unladylike behavior. Women may expect their husbands to be intensely interested in every word they say. Without question, women have been socialized to value interpersonal communications much more than men.

How does this affect marital communication? Men's communication role both reflects and reveals their power within marriage. Men tend to interrupt more than women. Women by contrast are more likely to ask questions, apologize, or elaborate in order to expand the conversation. Men speak with more certainty and intensity than women do. Women's voices have much more flexibility than men's. This gives them a greater range of tone for emotional expression. Sometimes, however, this quality is interpreted as whining and helpless. Not surprisingly, men tend to be more satisfied with the level of marital communication than women.

Traditional standards of gender-type behavior are changing. Alan Alda and Phil Donahue represent new masculine role models who are interested in women's thoughts and feelings and are supportive of women's new place in society. Women are also becoming more oriented to the business world with its emphasis on rational and unemotional analysis. These new patterns in our society may ultimately reshape marital communication styles. Even if this occurs, people will continue to have different learned patterns of communication. It is important to remember that these characteristic differences, whether or not they are gender related, are just that—differences.

Bridging Our Communication Differences

Often when married couples experience conflict, it is because they do not recognize that as two individuals they are bound to have differences. Instead they get caught up in who is right and who is wrong, or they compete to see who can change the other's way of thinking or behaving. Actually, social scientists believe that marital partners are drawn to each other as much by their differences as by their similarities. (Wouldn't it be awfully boring to be married to your clone?) In an open and accepting relationship, each partner makes distinct contributions to the marriage because of his/her differences.

How can characteristic differences in learned patterns of communication be turned into bridges to better communication? The first step is to identify your own characteristic patterns and assess how they are blocks to good communication in your marriage. Would modifying the pattern improve your relationship significantly? These are learned differences. They have been learned as a part of growing up. Because they are learned, they are not deterministic. That is, if you want to, you can change them. Deryl Fleming, a good friend and former pastor, once said in a sermon, "It is not that women are irrational and men are unemotional. It is that some men have learned to be unemotional and some women have learned to be irrational." Men who have difficulty communicating their emotions can learn to identify and talk about their feelings; women who get lost in their emotions can learn to focus more on their thoughts. And each can help the other.

In some ways we tend to reverse the stereotypes of male and female communicators. Preston communicates his feelings more quickly than Genie, but she is quicker to say what she is thinking. Recently, after working through a difficult issue, it became clear to us that part of Genie's frustration came from not knowing what Preston was thinking earlier in the discussion. His pattern is to wait until he has totally thought through an issue before sharing it. Realizing this happened fairly often, Genie asked him to try to verbalize his thoughts more readily. He agreed to work on doing that and asked Genie to help him by asking him more often, "What are you thinking about that right now?"

Through the years, Genie has had to work hard to identify

and communicate her feelings. We have found it helpful for Preston simply to ask, "What are you feeling about that?" Because we have agreed to help each other in the areas of our strength, we reduce the risk of being defensive when asked to communicate in a way that is not totally natural to us. We call this process *contracting* and will discuss it more in a later chapter.

(DB-13)

DEFENSIVENESS

Defensiveness may be the most difficult communication barrier to eliminate. When one or both partners become defensive, communication is almost always blocked.

Diverted Energy

Defensiveness is usually a result of having our self-esteem threatened. Effective communication is closely related to our feelings about ourselves. People who have relatively high feelings of self-esteem are characteristically responsive, sympathetic, empathetic, and express affection and affirmation easily. They are optimistic and cheerful and, thus, anticipate things going well. When things don't go well, they usually see it as a temporary difficulty which can be remedied. To the contrary, people who have relatively low self-esteem tend to expect failure and disappointment. They often expect slights, depreciation, and attacks. To protect themselves they often erect barriers of isolation and distrust and withdraw into apathy and loneliness.

The messages a husband and wife exchange with each other are far more important than those they exchange with anyone else. Almost anything one says or does has some effect on the self-esteem of the other, either raising or lower-

ing it. Generally, we are more self-disclosing to our partners than to anyone else and more dependent on their responses to build our self-image. Consequently, the chances of defensiveness are greater in marital communication.

Many messages between spouses include a request for approval. You trust your partner to use what s/he hears in your self-disclosures to help you feel good about yourself. Unfortunately, if s/he doesn't respond to your request for approval and recognition, you feel slighted. If s/he disagrees with you, you may feel rejected as though the core of your worth is symbolized by every word or deed you speak. At the slightest hint of the other's disinterest or disapproval, you are likely to respond with insecurity and defensiveness. When you feel that your thoughts, feelings, and opinions are not respected by those who matter to you, your defenses go up and productive conversation is almost impossible. Once threatened, your energy is diverted from understanding to defensiveness. Mutual trust is lost and along with it any chance for increasing your awareness of the other's point of view.

Here is an example of how defensiveness can block communication. Anne and Frank are both in their second marriage. They brought with them from their previous marriages ghosts of misunderstanding, lack of appreciation, and disrespect. One evening as Frank came in from work, Anne announced, "I've invited Joan and Ray over for dessert tonight." Frank exploded, "You know how tired I am after work. You never consider my feelings. You're always inviting people over without checking with me."

Perhaps Frank is right, and Anne should have checked with him first, but his defense of his right to participate in the decision puts Anne on the spot and raises her defenses. Now they will argue over whether Anne was thoughtless or Frank too rigid and have little chance to work out an agreement on how to plan their social life. They will both be so intent on defending their own egos that they cannot lower their guards enough to understand the other's point of view.

The Balm of Affirmation

Many of the problems in marriage can be traced to a sense of not being valued and appreciated. One way to bridge the gap of defensiveness is to consistently work at affirming the worth of our partner while at the same time valuing our own thoughts and feelings. We can do that by conveying respect for our partner's opinions, regardless of whether we agree or not. Remember that differences are a part of individuality and not an indication of disrespect. While we might not understand our partner's behavior or opinion, it helps to assume that, at least from his perspective, his reactions make sense. The task is to try to learn more about his point of view.

In the situation above, Frank had two choices. He could vent his feelings as he did, or he could try to solve the problem. When he responded defensively and vented his feelings, he got a defensive response from Anne. He might have gotten a constructive response had he offered a positive interpretation of her behavior followed by a request for change. For example, Frank might have said something like:

> Anne, I know you get tired of being cooped up in the house all day and really look forward to some adult company in the evening. And I appreciate your taking the initiative to arrange time with our friends. Sometimes, though, I'm really tired in the evenings and would like to be with just you. So I would like for you to check with me first before planning something for us.

Frank's recognition of her need and his positive observation are likely to minimize Anne's defensiveness. She is more likely to feel understood and appreciated and to hear his request for positive change. To help you learn more about how to avoid defensiveness we would like for you to do the following exercise.

Exercise G: Communicating Understanding, Respect, and Appreciation

1. Each of you will need a full-size sheet of paper divided in thirds. Write in the first section, "I feel understood when you . . ."; in the second section "I feel respected when you . . ."; and in the third, "I feel appreciated when you . . ."

2. Under each heading list three to five specific behaviors your partner does that cause you to feel understood, respected, and appreciated. When you have made your lists, share them with each other and give thanks.

3. Next, turn the sheet over and list three specific behaviors under each of the following headings: "To help me feel more understood I would like you to . . . "; "To help me feel more respected I would like you to . . ."; "To help me feel more appreciated I would like you to . . . ." You may find this hard to do. Some people have difficulty asking for what they want. We will talk more about this later when we discuss request making.

4. Now share your requests with each other. As you do so, think about your requests as gifts to your partner and to your relationship. Each of you will now know more specific ways to affirm and build positive feelings in each other and to decrease the possibility of defensiveness.

How can we build bridges rather than barriers? We can plan and spend time together; we can strive to understand and accept our differences; and we can build our partner's self-esteem through affirmation.

Chapter Three

WHAT TO SAY
AND HOW TO SAY IT

ONE OF THE MOST FREQUENT complaints we hear from couples about communication is, "My spouse won't talk to me." The usual rebuttal is, "I talk! Maybe not as much as you want. Or maybe I don't say what you want to hear. I really can't figure out what you want from me. What do you mean when you say we need to communicate more? What am I supposed to talk about?" The discussion usually ends here with one going off disappointed and the other bewildered.

We had this conversation ourselves many times. Genie pleaded with Preston to tell her about his everyday activities. He thought he did basically the same thing every day and could not figure out why she wanted him to repeat it for her. One day he had an especially exciting class session. Knowing that the other teachers in the department would not be particularly interested in his success, he stopped by Genie's office to tell her. He described vividly what he perceived had happened in class. He told her how pleased he was with the approach he had developed and the way the students responded to him. As he started telling her about what he wanted to try next, she could hold her excitement no longer and interrupted him, "That's it! That is what I've wanted to hear from you. I couldn't describe it before. I didn't want to just hear a replay of your day. I wanted to know what was happening to you. When I was begging you to talk to me more, I wanted you to share with me what was going on inside of you, what you were thinking and feeling about your day."

In this chapter we are going to try to answer the frustrated spouse's question, "What am I supposed to talk about?" As we discovered in the episode above, the most important thing we have to communicate to our partner is what is happening within us. In order to share that, however, I have to be aware of what is happening within me and know how to talk about it. In the first part of this chapter we are going to suggest some ways for increasing your self-awareness. In the second part we will provide some rules that will help you know how to communicate your awareness to your partner.

SELF-AWARENESS: THE MESSAGE WITHIN

If the most important message a person has to share with his partner is what is happening within him, he needs to take time to know himself. He must become aware of how he feels, what he thinks, what he wants and the sources of those feelings and thoughts. He also needs to be aware of his behavior: what he has done, is doing, or will do. Being aware of self is the beginning of good communication. But for many people, this is not a natural thing to do. Miller,

Nunnally, and Wackman in their book *Talking Together* created the awareness wheel as an aid to increasing self-awareness. The wheel has five parts: sensing, thinking, feeling, wanting, and acting. Each of these parts is equal, indicating that each part is equally important. Let's look at each part.

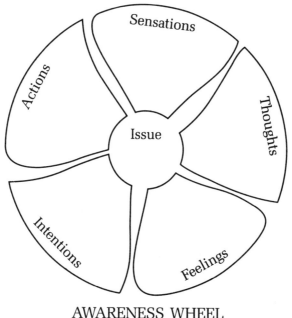

AWARENESS WHEEL

The "Awareness Wheel" is reprinted with permission from the authors of *Connecting with Self and Others*, 1988.
For more information, contact, Interpersonal Communication Programs, 7201 So. Broadway, Littleton, CO 80122.

Sensations have to do with what I take in from the outside world. They are based on my five senses: what I see, what I hear, what I smell, what I taste, and what I touch. For communication purposes we use what we see and hear more than the others. But all five are important. Think about entering a bakery and smelling cookies. What kinds of thoughts and feelings does that evoke? Maybe you think of visits to grandmother's house and have warm, loving feelings. Perhaps you think of your son's attempts at baking and feel proud of his accomplishments. Another way of thinking about sensations is that they are the raw data fed into our "computer." We take the outside world in through our senses, interpret it in our thoughts, and react to it with our feelings.

Thoughts are the second part of the awareness wheel. This part includes what I think, what I believe, and what my opinions are. That's the "computer" part of us. Sensations are the input, the data that I feed into my "computer." From that data I make interpretations, draw conclusions, and form opinions and beliefs. I see you sitting quietly with a frown on your face and hear you speak briskly to the children. I interpret what I saw and heard to mean you are angry, and I wonder if I have done something you did not like. I have taken in some information with my senses; I interpret that information and form my thoughts from it.

Emotions, the next part of the awareness wheel, are what I feel: excited, stimulated, loved, hurt, depressed. Remember, feelings are just that—and nothing more. Feelings are a God-given part of life—a part of our creation. They are our spontaneous reactions to our sensations and to the interpretations we make from them. Feelings can be painful, but without them life would hold little richness. Because they are spontaneous, we cannot *not* feel. We can deny the feeling. We can sometimes change the feeling by changing the way we think. We can ignore the feeling and decide to act differently from what we feel. But, we cannot *not* feel.

Feelings affect my thoughts, and my thoughts affect my feelings. When you think someone is angry with you, what kinds of emotions does that thought evoke? When you feel excited about going out with your partner tonight, what thoughts does that bring about?

You and your partner may experience feelings very differently. Some people tend to lean into their emotions and are very aware of them. They readily use them in determining what they want and in deciding what to do. Other people discount their feelings. John, an attorney, is very analytical and claims to deal only in facts. Feelings to him are not facts. In the courtroom, feelings may not be facts; but in human relations they are just as important as thoughts. In fact, research suggests that most people are more likely to act on the basis of their feelings than on the basis of their thoughts. If you identify with John, you may have to work harder to get in touch with your feelings. You may find that you have learned to hide your feelings not only from others but also from yourself. Getting in touch with your feelings does not mean that you have to give up your logical, analytical approach to life. Acknowledging your feelings does not mean being controlled by them. In fact, you may find you have more control because you can now decide whether you want to behave according to your thoughts or your feelings. You may also find that you have a much better understanding of your wants and actions.

Intentions are my wants, my wishes, my desires. They compose the fourth part of the wheel. "What do I want in this situation?" We are not talking about major goals or long-term plans, just this immediate situation, right now. "I really want to stay at home tonight, but I don't want to disappoint Genie. I want to let her know what I'm thinking, but I also want to do it in a way that will let her know I'm counting her interests for the evening."

Like feelings, people often refuse to acknowledge their wants, even to themselves. This may be because they associate wanting something for themselves as being selfish. If this is the way you feel, it may be helpful to be sure that you don't confuse "wants" with "demands." Selfishness may well enter in if intentions are thought of as demands. "I need it, so I am going to get it." "You have to do what I want." If that's what we think, then it is selfishness. But just being aware of what my wants are is not selfish.

Often rather than openly acknowledging our wants, we choose to manipulate. Sue is a good example. She has just discovered that the movie she wants to see will be shown for the last time tonight. But, it's also John's favorite night to watch television. She thinks of calling John at his office to tell him she wants to go to the movie but is afraid if she asks, he will say no. Instead, she devises another plan. Sue makes sure she gets home from work before John and changes into an outfit he particularly likes. When John finally arrives, the house is filled with the aroma of one of his favorite meals. Sue gives John lots of attention before and during dinner, and he is attentive and appreciative.

After the meal, Sue suggests John rest rather than help her with the dishes. He jumps at the chance, sits down in his favorite chair, switches on the TV and settles in for the evening. Sue soon joins him and at the first commercial mentions that one of her friends saw the film and really liked it. A little later she works into the conversation that this is the last night the film will be showing. As the hands of the clock move slowly around, Sue becomes more and more frustrated and angry. How could her husband be such an insensitive, selfish human being? She sits and stews in her anger until after the movie has begun. Eventually she finds something to pick a fight about with John in order to vent her frustration, disappointment, and anger. Sue's decision to manipulate rather than negotiate fails to achieve her goal and ends in a fight.

Why didn't Sue ask John directly for what she wanted? Sometimes people choose to manipulate rather than to communicate directly what they want simply because they think they know how their partners will respond. So, to avoid conflict or run the risk of being turned down, they try an indirect approach.

Others believe it is selfish to bluntly lay out their own needs or wants, preferring instead that their partners become aware of them on their own. Selfishness comes not from failing to recognize and to verbalize our own needs and desires but from behaving in ways that assure our needs and desires supersede those of others.

Rather than being selfish, openly letting our partners know our wants and needs in relation to them actually honors them by giving them the opportunity to choose whether or not to meet our needs. Had Sue told John she wanted to go to the movie, he then could have weighed his desire to stay home and watch television against Sue's desire to go to the movie. He might very well have chosen to take her, but on the other hand, he may have chosen not to. In either case, he at least would have had the chance to openly and knowingly make the choice.

In the scenario above, John never really had a choice. Additionally, if at first he had declined to go to the movies, he and Sue would have had the opportunity to discuss each other's position. Then, they could have attempted to negotiate in such a way that both of their needs would be met or at least they could have arrived at an understanding of one another's position. As it was, the choice to manipulate rather than to negotiate blocked John's chance to give his wife something she really wanted, their opportunity to learn more about each other, the possibility of sharing an enjoyable evening together, and in fact, resulted in the spat that Sue had feared in the very beginning.

If I am really aware of what my wants are, then I am not as likely to go "underground," or manipulate, to get them. Intentions actually help organize my behavior or actions. So if I am aware of my intentions, I can decide to behave in a way that guarantees that I get my way; or I can decide to negotiate fairly and be willing perhaps to give up a particular "want."

The fifth part of the wheel is *actions* or behavior. Not only do I need to be aware of thoughts or feelings, but I also need to know my actions—present, past, and future. Knowing that my palms are sweating might help me become more aware of a feeling. Being aware that I have been listening and not saying anything might help me understand my partner's response to my silence. Being aware of actions includes knowing what I have done, what I am doing now, and what I may do in the future.

The awareness wheel is most helpful when it is used to look at a particular issue or situation. You can use it to ask yourself, What am I thinking, feeling, wanting, doing, and

sensing in relation to this particular situation? People enter the awareness wheel at different points. A person may first be aware of his thoughts about an issue while his partner is first aware of her feelings. It does not matter where you start. What does matter is that you look at all five parts and become aware of what is happening to you in each area. Remember, the first and most important step in communicating with your partner is that you know yourself. Again, the most important information you have to give your partner is what is happening inside you.

Here is an example of how Preston used his awareness wheel recently. The issue was whether or not to attend a family wedding.

I know that the wedding is coming up, and I heard Genie say she thought we should go. I also know that the deadline for my project is getting close (sensations). I really tensed up and left the room when she said that (actions). I felt both frustrated and angry when she said that (feelings). I think she was pushing me to go. She doesn't really understand the pressure I'm feeling (thinking).

I really think I should go. I know the family will appreciate it and may even be hurt if I don't. Maybe I will be all right on the project (thinking). I hate this project. I feel so much pressure from it. I feel really close to these people and long to see them (feelings). I want to be with them (intentions), and I think I have an obligation to be with them (thinking). Even though I'm worried about the project (feelings), I am going to go. I'll probably fret some about it while I'm there, but I'll just live with it and keep it to myself. I'll tell Genie I can go (action).

Now it is your turn. We would like for you to do an exercise to practice using the awareness wheel.

Exercise H: Developing Self-Awareness

1. Think about something important, exciting, puzzling or in some other way meaningful that has happened to you recently—preferably in the last twenty-four hours. On a sheet of paper write the five parts of the awareness wheel—sensations, thoughts, feelings, intentions, and actions—leaving space under each. Now as you explore your awareness, write notes to yourself under the appropriate part of the awareness wheel. Remember, you don't have to go in any order.

2. When you are through, check to see that you have something under each heading. Which parts of your awareness were the most difficult to fill in? Do you need to explore further any one of the five areas?

3. When you are satisfied with your awareness in this situation, fold your paper and keep it for later. We will use it again after the next section.

SELF-DISCLOSURE

Now that I am aware of what is happening in me, what do I do with this information? First, if I know what I think, feel, sense, and want, I can then make a decision about what I want to tell my partner. It is not mandatory that I tell my partner every thought and feeling I have. It's not even wise to do so. Remember, in Chapter 1 we discussed the difference between totally open communication—expressing every thought and feeling that comes to mind—and measured communication. Research suggests that measured communication—carefully choosing what to say, and how and when to say it—has much more potential for building relationships.

Self-awareness increases my choices in selecting how much of myself to disclose. By using the skills of selective self-disclosure—sharing my sensations, thoughts, feelings—with another person, I gain her trust and increase the chance that she will be honest with me. The more I am willing to share myself, the more likely my partner will share herself with me. Thus we will have a better chance of understanding each other.

In our earlier discussion about attending the wedding, Preston told the family he wanted to talk about the trip. He told them about the various parts of his awareness. He purposefully left out the part about being angry at Genie because he no longer felt angry after processing the whole situation. Afterwards, the others were better able to understand his previous reluctance to talk about it, his mixture of feelings, and confusion about what he wanted to do. Each talked about his own awareness, and together they decided to go. When Preston got quiet during the trip or seemed to withdraw, the rest of the family understood.

Rules for Self-Disclosure
With self-awareness and the decision to share this awareness, what is the best way for me to convey my thoughts and feelings to my partner? How can I say what I want to say so that my partner can hear me and understand me and not feel defensive? Let's look at several rules for self-expression.

• The Speaking-for-Self Rule
The first rule for self-expression in every communication system we have ever reviewed is the use of "I" statements rather than "you" statements. "You" statements tend to blame the hearer and thus cause defensiveness; by contrast, "I" statements indicate the speaker's ownership of the thoughts and feelings expressed. For example, I might say, "I

feel hurt," rather than, "You hurt me." Or, "I like for you to tell me when you will be home," rather than, "You should let me know when you will be home." Can you feel the difference the "I" statements make? Owning my thoughts and feelings by using "I" statements reduces the chances of my partner's feeling defensive about what I am telling him. "You" statements mean my partner must defend himself against my accusations, whereas "I" statements are no more than my own opinions, feelings, or desires.

The authors of *Talking Together* refer to this as the "speaking-for-self" rule. We like that designation better than just referring to the "I" rule because it gets to the reason behind the rule. The real purpose is to take full responsibility for what is coming out of me. A statement that begins, "I think you ought . . . ," although technically using "I", is not really speaking for one's self; it is still an over-responsible "you" statement. Instead, the phrase, "I wish you would think about . . . ," reflects the spirit of speaking for self.

• The Statement Rule

As I self-disclose, making statements is much better than asking questions. If I can say, "I was really worried about you last night," rather than, "Why didn't you call me?" my partner will understand how I felt in that situation and will again respond to me through understanding rather than in a defensive manner.

A helpful way to know what to talk about is to build your self-disclosure around awareness wheel statements. Making statements that relate to each part of the awareness wheel—sensation statements, thought statements, feeling statements, intention statements, and action statements—provides your partner with a complete message that leads to better understanding. Leaving one part out leaves a gap in understanding.

Two areas of the awareness wheel that are most difficult to share are feelings and intentions. Even after we are aware of our own feelings and intentions, it is very difficult to decide to share those with our partner. All areas of the awareness wheel are important. If any one is omitted, understanding is more difficult. Knowing my partner's feelings and intentions on an issue greatly increases my ability to understand his thoughts and actions. Feelings and intentions add color to my self-disclosure. My partner may be aware of my logical thinking concerning an issue, but if I am not willing to tell her how I feel and what I want, she has no way of knowing what effects those thoughts have on my emotions and intentions. In terms of understanding each other, my feelings and intentions are probably much more important to the understanding process than are my thoughts or my sensations. If you can understand what I feel and want in any situation, then you may be able to deal with it better. Feelings and wants are facts in our relationship with each other. If I feel something, then for me that's real and it has to be taken into consideration. When I tell my partner what I feel, I become vulnerable; and perhaps this vulnerability is what makes it hard to reveal my feelings.

Joanna and Roger are a two-career couple in a large city. They have been married for five years and are both in management positions in their companies. They have given each other freedom to grow in their careers and have not had restrictive rules for one another. One morning as they left for their offices, Roger told Joanna that he had a rather easy afternoon scheduled and planned to be at home by half past five. Joanna said she would be home soon after that. Roger agreed to prepare the grill and to cook dinner for them. They were both delighted at the prospect of a quiet evening together in the middle of the week.

As Roger prepared to leave that afternoon, one of his fellow managers came by his office to discuss a new idea he wanted to implement. Roger listened impatiently for a while, but as his co-worker talked, Roger began to get excited about his idea. Another associate joined them, and they continued to discuss the plan and how they might implement it. Several times Roger started to excuse himself to call Joanna, but another idea would surface, and he could not get away. Finally, about eight o'clock the discussion ended, and Roger left for home.

As he drove into his driveway, he pushed the remote control to open the garage door. When the door opened, there was Joanna, standing in the garage with her hands on her hips. He knew there was going to be a scene! Before Roger was out of his car, Joanna began to tell him he had ruined her evening. She said he should have called her so she would not have had to wait all evening. He told her that he did not have to report to her any more than she had to report to him. They had given each other the freedom needed to develop their careers, and he needed that freedom tonight when he and his colleagues were discussing new strategies for their business. They argued and argued about who was right, what was fair, and what their responsibilities were to one another.

Finally, exhausted from their argument they both fell silent. Joanna looked at Roger and said, "I was so scared! I guess I never told you about a night when I was ten years old. My daddy didn't come home to dinner that night. He still wasn't home when I went to bed, and I was really afraid. The next morning the doorbell rang, and the coroner was there to tell us that Daddy had been killed in an accident the night before. Roger, I was so afraid something terrible had happened to you."

Roger took her in his arms and held her for a long time. "I will never make you wonder what has happened to me again. I had no idea that you would be that worried. I've come home this late other nights. But from now on, no mat-

ter what I am doing or who is in my office, if you are expect-
ing me, I will call you. I don't want you to be afraid."
Although he still believed it was important to be available to
his business associates and to have freedom to explore ideas
as needed, he also had a better understanding of Joanna because she was willing to share her feelings with him.

Intentions are also difficult to share. Some of the same
reasons that hinder our becoming aware of our intentions

make it even harder to share them with a partner. No one wants to be seen as demanding or selfish. Wants and intentions do not have to be demands. Stating intentions is simply saying what I would like to have happen in this particular situation. That does not mean I am demanding that the results be what I desire. I am just saying, "This is what I would like; let's talk about it. I'd also like to know what you want."

Intentions or requests usually sound better to both the speaker and the hearer if they are expressed as "wants" and not as "needs." For example, "I want to have the family together tonight." Not, "I need to have the family together." Do you hear the difference? If my partner says she needs something, I am more likely to hear that as a demand. However, if my partner says she wants something, I hear that as a desire. We can negotiate desires much easier than we can negotiate needs.

Some people find it difficult to make requests of their spouse. Often this is because the person does not feel worthy or good about self. Unfortunately, such feelings often lead to the decision to manipulate rather than to ask directly for what is wanted. If this happens to you, try thinking of your request as a gift to your spouse. Knowing what you want relieves your partner from having to figure it out alone. Also, it is more fun to give because you want to than because you have to. Remember, when Jesus said, "Love your neighbor as yourself" (Mark 12:33, NIV), he was instructing us to care for both our neighbor (wife/husband) and ourselves.

• Question Rules

While it is true that statements are best for facilitating interpersonal communication, questions are sometimes needed. When questions are needed, keep in mind two rules that will improve communication effectiveness and help prevent problems. First, when you need to ask a question, make a statement before you ask the question. In other words, disclose something about yourself before you ask your partner to disclose. "I'd like to go to the movies tonight. How do you feel about that?" or "I am really frightened because our savings have dwindled. What can we do to cut our spending?" When I disclose something about how I am reacting to a situation before I ask my partner a question, he is much more likely to be self-disclosing to me without getting defensive.

The second rule is to avoid *why* questions. When asking a question, concentrate on asking how, when, what; but try to avoid why. What is the purpose of avoiding *why* questions? The word *why* tends to create defensiveness in people. It makes us feel put on the spot, probably because it recalls for us the times that parents asked, "Why did you do that?" Many times we had no earthly idea why we had done what we did—we just did it. *Why* questions are appropriate in the classroom or office where the emphasis is on facts and logical analysis. However, in interpersonal relations where feelings and intentions are important to understanding, logical explanations may simply not be possible. Feelings particularly are not guided by the canons of logic. They just are! In marital communication, trying to force logical explanations when a partner is unable to explain usually ends with his feeling discounted. Reframing the *why* question using a *who, when, where,* or *how* will often get the same information without the risk of defensiveness. "What did you think when I was late?" is a much better question than, "Why did you call my office looking for me?"

• The Now Rule
The process of developing awareness often stirs up material from the past and thoughts and feelings unrelated to the issue or situation at hand. It is helpful to follow the "now rule" in selecting what to disclose. The "now rule" requires

the conversation to remain in the present. When you tell your partner about a situation, be sure to talk only about that particular issue. Do not bring up issues from the past or circumstances that have little to do with the current problem. Stay with what is happening with you and your partner right now. That usually provides enough to discuss without bringing up situations that occurred last month or three years ago and perhaps never were settled. It is important to settle past issues, but do that at another time.

Remember Preston's issue related to the wedding? He perceived Genie's suggestion to go as pressure on him to do something he was still not sure about. That caused him to feel angry toward her. He decided, however, not to bring that into the discussion about the wedding because it was not related to the issue at hand. He did bring it up later when he and Genie was discussing the kinds of behaviors that often spark anger in them.

Exercise I: Using Self-Disclosure

1. With these rules for self-disclosure in mind, let's go back to the exercise we worked on earlier. Look at it again in relation to all parts of the awareness wheel. Is there anything you want to add to any area?
2. When you are satisfied with your awareness, think about how you can tell your partner what you have written. Remember the importance of "I" statements and sharing from all five parts of the awareness wheel. We think you will be more spontaneous if you do not look at what you wrote. It has served its purpose in increasing your awareness, and may actually get in the way of conversation at this point.
3. Now, turn to your partner and take turns telling him/her about your awareness of this situation.

Chapter Four

AVOIDING MISUNDERSTANDING

ONE EVENING as Preston was preparing an omelet for dinner, he asked Genie, "Don't you think some of your bran muffins would be good with dinner tonight?" Genie, who was reading in an adjoining room, enthusiastically agreed. Thirty minutes later Preston asked, "When will the muffins be ready, Genie?" Genie was totally surprised. She had no idea that he had expected her to make muffins for the meal. Preston was upset because he thought his question implied he wanted her to come to the kitchen to make muffins. Genie, however, thought he was simply asking if she would like to have muffins with the omelet. We had a complete misunderstanding of the meaning of Preston's question.

In Chapter 1, we identified understanding as the primary goal of communication. Husbands and wives particularly need effective communication to bridge the gap between their individuality and increase their understanding of each other. Unfortunately, in most interpersonal communication the chance of *misunderstanding* seems to be greater than the chance of *understanding.* In this chapter, we will discuss some ways to increase the odds for understanding. It is probably impossible to avoid all misunderstanding, but if the sender and the receiver assume responsibility for clarifying meaning, understanding is possible. We want to emphasize this principle: communication which leads to understanding is the responsibility of both the speaker and the hearer. Blaming your partner for misunderstandings will not do. Both must accept the potential of misunderstanding and assume responsibility for avoiding it.

In this chapter, we will first discuss some factors which interfere with understanding. Then we will present some skills that both the sender and receiver can use to increase the chances that message sent equals message received. In the last part of the chapter, we will focus on the importance of choosing the right style for communicating a message.

UNDERSTANDING VS. MISUNDERSTANDING

How does misunderstanding occur? Part of the answer lies in the fact that the message we want to convey to our partner originates inside us. The message is not the words we say. It is the feelings, thoughts, and intentions that well up within us. These thoughts and feelings must be translated into words before they can be conveyed to a receiver. In any act of communication, there are essentially three elements: the sender within whom the message develops, the message itself, and the receiver who must hear the message and translate it into his or her own awareness.

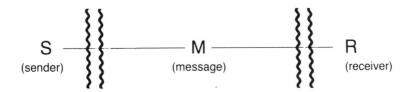

This process is reflected in the diagram above. The goal, of course, is to assure that the message generated within the sender is the same message that is understood by the receiver. This seems so simple, but if you consider the actual dynamics of communication, we think you will see why it is more likely that the message sent will not equal the message received. Let's look at this process.

We are all self-protecting. The message within me is a part of me; and when I attempt to convey that message, I become vulnerable. We each want to present ourselves in the very best light. Consequently, I am likely to censor any message that comes out of my mouth in order to protect my vulnerable spots and present myself in the best way possible. The wiggly lines represent these censors in the diagram. The censors may garble the message I am trying to send and decrease my receiver's ability to understand the real message within me. For example, my child asks permission to do something. I am fearful for the child and want to protect her. On the other hand, I don't want to be seen as a bad, controlling parent. What I feel is *No* because I'm afraid; what I think is *Yes, she probably should be allowed to do it;* and what I actually say is, "Maybe."

The second element in the process is the message itself. In order to communicate the message that is within me, I must translate it into words. The censors discussed above influence our choice of words, but the words themselves are only symbols for the meanings within us. Because they are only symbols, they have different meanings for different people. The picture a word conveys for the husband may not be the same picture the wife sees. For example, the word *chair* is a symbol for a piece of furniture. When you hear the word *chair,* what comes to mind? A straight-backed chair? A recliner? A comfortable, overstuffed chair? A desk chair? The word *chair* brings a different picture to each of us.

Using words to symbolize feelings is even more difficult. When I use the word *depressed* to symbolize a feeling, what does that bring to your mind? Some people picture someone who is blue and temporarily sad over some situation. Another person may picture someone crying, chronically withdrawn, and unwilling to communicate with anyone. The fact that we must use words as symbols for our thoughts and feelings greatly increases the chance of misunderstanding.

Words create problems in understanding not only because they convey different pictures, but also because they generate different emotions. For most people, the word *mother* carries with it a feeling of love, acceptance, generosity, and warmth. However, to a person who had an abusive mother, the word may carry with it feelings of rejection, hurt, and jealousy. If, in trying to convey the message within me to my listener, I choose a word that has positive feelings associated with it for me but has very negative emotions associated with it for the receiver, the chances of understanding will again be reduced.

Finally, before the message can be understood, it must pass through a second set of censors. Not only does the sender censor the message before it is projected, the hearer also has a set of censors that further complicate the understanding of the message. These censors grow out of the situation in which the communication takes place: the past and present relationship between the sender and receiver, the context of the situation (for example, who else is present), and a variety of other social and psychological factors. Sometimes, this means that the receiver hears only what he wants to hear. At other times, it means that he or she hears what was already anticipated. And at other times, it may mean that it is heard and interpreted in a way that will be most advantageous to that person. So not only the words of a message convey different meanings to the sender and the receiver, but the censorship of the sender and receiver may also result in different messages.

The sender or receiver who has examined his self-awareness is much better equipped to send or receive an accurate message. Also, keeping in mind just how complicated the communication process is, and actually anticipating misunderstanding to occur, is helpful. Blaming the misunderstanding on each other will not help. Both partners need to acknowledge that the words your ears hear are not necessarily the words that my lips spoke, and that the words my lips spoke are not necessarily the message within me that I want you to understand. With this in mind let's now look at some specific skills to help improve understanding.

ACTIVE LISTENING

Listening is more than maintaining a polite silence while rehearsing in your mind the speech you are going to make as soon as you get an opening. Have you ever found yourself in this position: silently rehearsing in your mind what you are going to say next when your partner stops talking? Passive silence is not the same as listening. Active listening is hard work and requires paying close attention to what the speaker is saying and doing. Good listeners also communicate their interest in what is being said and their acceptance of the speaker in a way that encourages him or her to continue the self-disclosure.

Exercise J: Identifying Good Listening Skills

Think of a person to whom you like to talk. This is probably a person who is a good listener. Make a list of the reasons you like to talk to this person. What does she do while you talk to her? Now think of a person to whom you find it difficult to talk. What does this person do that makes it hard to talk to her? Share both of your lists with your partner; then see if your good listener uses some of the following listening skills.

Nonverbal Listening Skills

A good listener looks at the sender and maintains eye contact with him. He doesn't look around at other activities or other people but looks at the sender and conveys the idea that he is giving the sender his full attention. The listener may nod, smile, frown or provide other appropriate nonverbal responses while the other person speaks. He may lean toward the person rather than sitting back in his chair. When the listener makes a conscious effort to get up and turn off the television set or to put down the newspaper or book he is reading, he is saying, "You are important to me, and I want to hear and understand what you have to say." Not only do the listener's nonverbal behaviors help the sender feel cared about and that what he is saying is important, they also help the listener himself concentrate on what the sender is saying.

We have a friend who always greets us as we enter the hall at church. Every Sunday she is there to say hello, and we always feel that she is glad we are there. "How was your week?" she asks. But as we begin to tell her what has happened since last Sunday, we see her eyes wandering up and down the hall. She is looking for the next person she is going to greet. Our desire to continue the conversation at that point dies. She really doesn't care how our week was or what has happened since we last saw her. The initial feeling of warmth disappears when we realize from her nonverbal behaviors that she is not listening.

Avoiding Interrupting

A good listener also waits for the other person to complete a message rather than interrupting to express his own ideas. He is truly concentrating on what the sender is saying rather than looking for a place to jump in with his opinions and beliefs or with a comparable story from his experience. The listener gives the sender time to complete the story or message without interruptions.

To avoid interrupting it is helpful to ask the speaker if he or she is ready for your response. Sometimes it is hard to interpret pause or silence. It may be a signal the speaker is finished and ready for a response. But it may be that he or she is just taking time to think about what to say next or how to say it. Don't rush silences. It takes time to explore one's awareness and to choose the right skills to use in self-expression. Good communication takes time and cannot be rushed. A good listener gives his partner plenty of time to finish her message before beginning his own response.

Questioning as an Aid to Listening

Questioning the sender is a listening skill that needs to be cultivated. Your partner knows you are listening when you ask thoughtful questions. A good question tells the other person you are really listening, and not just thinking of what you are going to say next. Remember, however, that questions can produce defensiveness so the listener must be careful about how the questions are asked. Again, be careful of *why* questions. Ask instead questions that begin with *how, when, where,* and *what.*

The awareness wheel can be used to know what questions to ask. Developers of the awareness wheel call this skill "checking out." The checking-out skill is asking questions

about the five areas of the awareness wheel. Instead of saying, "I feel, I think, I want," you simply ask a question: "What did you see when you began to think about that?" "What are you feeling about that situation?" "What do you want to happen?" This skill is a way of asking your partner for more information about what is happening in her awareness wheel. It is also a way of encouraging your partner to explore all parts of her awareness and to share that with you.

We discussed in the last chapter that talking about feelings adds color to a person's self-disclosure. Feeling statements give a dimension to the message that provides valuable information for the receiver. So listening for feeling words is a way the receiver can strive to better understand the sender's message. Since feeling messages are so powerful, listening for them is very important.

Many times we have had one partner in a marriage say he really wants to communicate at a deeper level, but has difficulty getting the other partner to talk. The checking-out skill works well to encourage the quieter partner to be aware of what is happening to her and also to talk about more of her awareness wheel. This is most effective when the more verbal partner first models good self-disclosure and then uses the checking-out skill. "John, I'm feeling a bit uneasy about our plans for the weekend." (feeling statement) "How are you feeling about them?" (checking-out skill)

Stuart suggests using the "two-question rule" as a means of improving listening skills and assuring your partner of your interest.

Husband: "How was your day?"
Wife: "Oh, not so good. My boss tried to tell me how to direct my new project."
Husband: "What do you want to do with the project?"

Husband: "What did you do today?"
Wife: "The children had so many places to go today I spent the day in the car."
Husband: "How do you feel about that?"

This skill involves asking a question, listening to the answer, and then asking a second question that follows from the answer you heard. Your partner will know that you listened to what she said if you ask a second related question. Your partner will be encouraged to tell you more when she perceives that you are interested enough to ask another question about what she has told you. Additionally, to ask the second question you have to listen well.

Two words of caution about questions. First, as you ask questions, be sure to ask only the questions that will help you better understand your partner's message. Do not ask questions that tend to fix blame for the situation. Second, do not overuse questions. Some people communicate only through questions. We call these people "grand inquisitors." Questions are valuable when used to get additional information about your partner, but be sure that you also give your partner information about yourself as well.

The use of these listening skills can increase understanding greatly. How do you and your partner rate as listeners? Which of these skills are you aware of using already? Which skills do you want to develop? Let's do an exercise to evaluate your present use of these skills and to contract with each other on how to improve your listening skills.

Exercise K: Evaluating Our Listening Skills

1. Each partner take a sheet of paper and make a list of the things you try to do to make it easy for your partner to talk to you. Now make a list of the things your partner does that make it easy for you to talk to him. Be sure to keep your lists positive. When you have completed your lists, turn to each other and take turns telling your partner what you have listed. Again, be sure to be positive in your discussion.
2. Now list some things you would like for your partner to do that would make it easier for you to talk to him/her. Again share these with your partner.
3. Finally, look at each other's list of "wants." Decide on two from the list that you are willing to try to do during the next week and tell your partner which ones they are.

PARROTING AND PARAPHRASING

Two additional skills husbands and wives can use to increase the likelihood of understanding are parroting and paraphrasing. These skills are designed specifically to be certain that message sent equals message received. That is, they are used when you want to be sure that the message inside the sender is the message the listener understands. Both require the sender to use good self-disclosure skills and the listener to use good listening skills.

Parroting is saying back to your partner exactly what s/he said to you. Sender: "I will meet you at the front door of the cafeteria at seven o'clock." Receiver: "I'm to meet you at the front door of the cafeteria at seven." Sender: "That's right." Parroting is particularly helpful when understanding directions such as when to meet, how to do a task, or where to go.

Paraphrasing is a much more complicated skill. It is also repeating your partner's message, but in a different way. Paraphrasing involves saying what you understood your partner to say in your own words. Using your own words rather than the exact words of the speaker avoids the problems associated with the different meanings of words we discussed earlier. Rather than repeating your partner's words, you repeat what you understood from those words.

This is not a skill that you would want to use with every message from your partner. It is a skill to be used with important or complicated messages. Developers of the awareness wheel we discussed earlier describe paraphrasing as a three-step process which they call "shared meaning." First, the sender alerts the receiver that this is an important message. He begins his message by saying, "I have something important to tell you, and I really want to be sure you understand me. When I'm finished, I'd like for you to tell me what you understood me to say." In other words the sender puts a "red flag" on the message. It is not fair to send the message and then say, "Now tell me what I said." That's like saying, "I've got you now. I knew you weren't listening to me." So tell the listener when your message is important to you and when you want to have it paraphrased. After the sender gives the message, the listener repeats what s/he understood. The sender then confirms or clarifies the message. He says, "Yes, you've got it; that's it." That's confirming. Or you might say, "Well, you got the first part. Let me try the last part again." Or you might say, "No, that's not what I meant. Let me try again." Or, "You got what I am thinking, but I'm not sure you really understand how I feel or what I want." If the listener did not get the entire message, the sender tries again until he can say, "Now I think you have it all." The sender sends a message to the receiver, the receiver repeats the message in his own words, and the sender confirms or clarifies the paraphrase.

Several words of caution about paraphrasing. Keep the message brief. It may be necessary to send several messages before the entire meaning is given. Cover two or three parts of the awareness wheel in one message, but no more. Since the process depends on your receiver to paraphrase what you say, if you give him too much at one time, he will not be able to remember the entire message. So use several shorter messages until the entire message has been sent.

Next, the receiver cannot add anything of his own to the message. He simply gives the message back to the sender. When the first portion of the message is understood, the sender says, "Okay, that's it. Now let me give you some more." The sender may do two or three or four of these until the message is complete. The receiver may then say, "I need to tell you what's happening with me now. Let me be the sender." Then you change roles. Be sure, however, that you agree when you change roles. It is most important that you both know what your role is to be.

This process may sound slow and tedious. And it is! It definitely slows down communication. That is in itself good. Effective communication takes time. However, in reality it is more efficient than normal communication because it avoids misunderstanding. This is a difficult skill, but one we have found to pay great dividends in improving our marital communication. It takes practice and a strong desire to better understand your partner, but it is worth the effort.

GIVING POSITIVE AND NEGATIVE FEEDBACK

Wouldn't it be wonderful if all we ever felt for our marital partner's behavior was excitement and approval? Even in the best marriages, partners feel irritated by the behavior of the other. Some of these are minor irritations and probably ought to be ignored. But some, even small ones, eventually begin to affect the relationship and need to be dealt with. Feedback is the way a couple expresses reactions to each other's behavior. Misunderstandings often occur either because feedback is withheld, or it is given in inappropriate ways.

All of the skills and rules you have learned thus far are applicable to giving both positive and negative feedback. Three additional rules are particularly important in providing information to your partner about how his/her behavior is affecting you. If misunderstanding is to be reduced, that information should always be *selective, specific,* and *timely.*

Feedback should be mostly positive and focused on behavior that can be changed. One author suggests that for every negative comment, a person should receive at least ten positives. Feedback that is vague or comes long after the behavior has occurred has little benefit. Telling your partner how good a job she did without telling her what you liked about it or telling her you did not like what she did days later does little to bring about positive change.

Positive Feedback

When feedback is given, it is often negative. Researchers have shown that husbands and wives are far more likely to give each other negative feedback than are unmarried partners. Unfortunately, it has also been shown that parents and disturbed adolescents exchange high rates of negative feedback. For some people it is more difficult to express positive feelings about a person they love than it is to make negative comments. And it is also true that for some, receiving positive comments is more difficult than receiving negative ones. Again, researchers have shown that positive feedback is much more likely to bring about positive change in behavior than is negative. Marital partners have a powerful influence on each other's feelings of self-worth; consequently, it is important that they frequently communicate to each other how much they care for and appreciate each other. Just being aware inside yourself is not enough. Your partner cannot crawl inside your skin and know how much you cherish him. He can only know if you tell him. Let's use an exercise to practice doing that.

Exercise L: Giving Positive Feedback

1. On separate sheets of paper, each of you list at least five things your partner does that make a positive contribution to your relationship. For example, Preston listed: takes care of paying bills and balancing the checkbook, snuggles with me, pays attention to my parents, compliments me on my appearance, gives me lots of pats and hugs.
2. Husbands go first sharing your list with your partner. Use good "I" statements: "I appreciate . . ." or, "I think you contribute a lot to our relationship by the way you . . . ." Be sure to use only positives and avoid qualifiers such as, "I like the way you cook, *but I wish you would do it more often,*" or, "Sometimes you . . . ." Be as specific as possible. Instead of, "I like your care for the children," try, "I was pleased when I saw you being so patient with the children's questions last night." Lots of examples will also help you be specific.
3. Wives, you will be the receivers. Use the listening

skills you have learned. This is also a good place to practice paraphrasing. After each of the positive items your husband identifies, paraphrase your understanding of his comment. For example, after Preston has identified the first item on his list, Genie might say, "You really appreciate the way I handle the details of our day-to-day finances."

4. When the husband has exhausted his list, switch roles so that the wife becomes the sender and the husband the receiver.

Negative Feedback

We hope the above exercise was a good experience for you. Being aware of and communicating positive feelings frequently make it easier when you must share things with your partner that he or she is not going to be as happy about hearing. Looking for and using opportunities to give positive feedback to my partner make it easier for him to hear negative comments. Be careful, however, not to give positive feedback *only* when it is to be followed by negative. That approach will devalue the positive feedback and cause your partner to become defensive as soon as he hears a positive comment. Positive feedback needs to be well-distributed throughout your daily interaction.

It does help, however, to begin with some positives before launching into the negative. "John, I really appreciate your cleaning up for me after dinner. I was tired and needed some time to myself. Thanks a lot. I think a part of the reason I was so tired was that I was really upset with you for being so late coming home from work again tonight. I feel like I never know when to have dinner ready. I really wish you would call me if you are going to be later than six-thirty."

Notice that the wife in the example above was specific and focused on the behavior that was bothering her and not on her partner's personality. Using descriptions of behavior rather than judgments on personal traits helps to keep defensiveness at a minimum. If you tell me about my behavior, I can change that; but if you are critical of me as a person, I may not think I can change. It is much better to say, "I don't like all the clutter in the living room," than to say, "You are a slob." I can pick up the clutter, but what can I do about being a slob?

Again, in the dialogue above, not only does the wife not attack her husband personally ("You are so inconsiderate"), but she also uses good self-disclosure skills and makes a specific request for change. She expresses her concern and request for change in a timely fashion. She could have held her dislike for his lateness for several weeks while withdrawing more and more from the relationship. Instead she voiced her concern and suggested a change in behavior that would have an immediate and positive effect. Request with a future orientation like, "I'd like for you to go to church with me next Sunday," is far more likely to bring about the desired effect than, "You never go to church with me."

The following set of rules from Richard Stuart's *Helping Couples Change*[1] summarizes what we have been saying about feedback statements:

1. They should begin with "I."
2. They should refer to specific behaviors.
3. They should stress the positives in the behaviors, and if not positives, they should be phrased as requests for positive and specific changes.
4. They should be expressed as soon after the focal behaviors as possible—so that the feedback is present-oriented.
5. They should be offered at a proper time and in a way that is most likely to be received.

---

[1]Richard Stuart, *Helping Couples Change* (Champaign: Research Press, 1980), p. 233.

HOW TO SAY IT:
STYLES OF COMMUNICATION

As we have seen, understanding is influenced by the content of the message we send and how we listen to our partner's message. But the message is not all to be considered. How the message is expressed is also important to understanding. Let's look at the way or the style in which messages may be expressed.

Miller, Nunnally, and Wackman in *Talking Together* discuss four styles of communication that are identified by the intention and behavior of the speaker. All four styles are useful and appropriate in various situations. The speaker should be aware of what s/he wants and choose the style that best fits that intention.

Style One consists of sociable, friendly, day-to-day conversation. There is little self-disclosure in this style. It allows for planning, giving information, joking, reporting, describing, visiting, and expressing preferences. The intentions of the speaker in this style are to keep things on an even keel. No change is desired. Some examples of this style are "I'd rather go to the movie." "The store opens at nine in the morning." "I am sleepy." "I went by the dry cleaners." "Your shirt is in the washer." It is relaxed chitchat.

Style Two has entirely different intentions. In this style the speaker wants to be in control. It includes giving instructions, advising, selling, blaming, complaining, criticizing, and other attempts to control. In this style the speaker wants the situation to turn out in a specific way and attempts to make change or to resist change. In this style the partner's feelings, wants, and intentions are not considered. The speaker may try to enforce his own wants through persuasion or force. "You" statements are common in this style.

Misunderstanding, distance, and tension may result from its use; however, style two has value when used correctly. Good use of this style includes: giving directions ("Meet me at six-thirty at the grocery store"), advising ("It would be hard to do it that way"), praising ("You did a great job with the children"). Poor use of this style includes: blaming ("It's your fault"), complaining ("I always have to do your part"), accusing ("You didn't do the dishes again"). Although this style has a useful purpose, it is extremely important that it be used with care and only when it can be used properly.

Style Three is one of speculation. It is used when the speaker wants to examine a situation, to explore alternatives, or to reflect on what has happened. The speaker is looking at the past or into the future. "I wonder if being tired contributed to our argument last night?" "Maybe I could find time to get some rest after work." "Perhaps we could explore the possibility of outside help." "I probably was thinking about the office situation." In this style, speaking for self and questions are used. It is used when there is an issue to be examined; little emotion is expressed, and no commitments are made for action. It gives an opportunity to look at what has happened and what may happen in the future. In this style, the thinking section of the awareness wheel is the part that is used most.

Style Four is present oriented. All parts of the awareness wheel are used. The speaker is aware of self as well as partner and uses all the skills we have discussed. This style is used when the speaker wants to work on an issue and is willing to be cooperative, trusting of partner, and ready to make himself vulnerable. It is a working style and should only be used in situations that need serious attention. It is recognized by the inclusion of all parts of the awareness wheel: "I feel satisfied about the way we decided to divide our responsibilities in the kitchen. I want to give it a try for a while. I think it will work, and I am excited about the possibilities." This style is particularly good for giving feedback and has considerable power for relationship building. It is an excellent style for husbands and wives to use in working on issues and to express their love, respect, and appreciation for each other. It is a very intense style, however, and not one to be used all the time.

Again, all four styles are useful. The skill rests in choosing the proper style for your intention. If I want to give you direction, I choose the second style. If I want to explore the possibilities of a situation, I choose the third. If I want to visit with you about your day, I use the first style. If I want to tell you about my wants, feelings, intentions, actions, and sensations, I use the fourth. We have found in problem solving that we often move back and forth between the third and fourth styles. We identify our present concerns, thoughts, and observations in style four. We discuss how we got to where we are (history or background) in style three and explore possible solutions (future). Then we go back to four to again express our current thoughts, feelings, and wants about the possibilities and finally commit to a solution.

Communication that increases understanding increases the potential for an enriched marriage. For most couples, understanding is far more important than agreement. In this chapter we have identified skills that can be used by the sender or receiver to increase the likelihood of understanding. Because misunderstanding is so easy, probably the most serious mistake either of you could make is to blame the other for a misunderstanding. Misunderstandings are going to occur, but they can be reduced and overcome if both partners assume responsibility for doing everything possible to achieve understanding.

Chapter Five

USING COMMUNICATION SKILLS TO RESOLVE CONFLICT

W E VISITED RECENTLY with a couple who had participated in one of our workshops. "You know, we are really making progress with those communication skills we learned. I think we understand each other much better now," John said.

"The skills still feel a bit awkward," Jan continued, "but I push myself to use them; and I hear John using them more and more in our conversations."

"And the more I use them, the more natural they feel," John confirmed. "But, I still have problems in one area. I use the skills just fine until I get angry. When we really start to get into it, I forget all I've learned about good communication."

John's admission is one we hear often. Probably nothing blocks communication quicker than anger. Yet, nowhere in marital interaction is communication needed more than when tempers rise. In those situations we have noticed that people tend to act in one of two ways. Some simply clam up, withdraw into themselves, and say nothing. These people we call "stuffers." Others demonstrate their anger by shouting whatever comes to mind with little regard for how it comes out. These people we call "yellers." We know these types well. Genie tends to be a stuffer and Preston a yeller. Painfully, we discovered neither approach leads to an enriched marriage.

Many marriages fail because people are unable to handle anger well. In this chapter, we want to focus on ways you can use communication skills to help you more effectively handle marital conflict and the anger that results from it. Conflict need not be a destructive force in a relationship. When handled properly, it can be a creative force for relationship growth.

Before going further we would like for you to assess your typical approach to dealing with conflict. The exercise below is designed to help you do that.

Exercise M: How We Deal with Conflict

1. Each of you will need a separate sheet of paper numbered from one to twenty. Place an *X* beside the number of the statement below if you believe it is true of the way you handle disagreements.
   1. Try to negotiate
   2. Withdraw—no action
   3. Threaten violence
   4. Behave violently
   5. Blame partner saying "you never . . ." or "you always . . ."
   6. Blame someone else
   7. Give in
   8. Threaten divorce or separation
   9. Assign winning more importance than listening

10. Pretend not to understand
11. Apologize prematurely
12. Attempt to rationalize away the anger
13. Sulk or pout
14. Openly face the issue
15. Avoid the real issue
16. Fear conflict with partner
17. Am ready to kiss and make up soon after a disagreement
18. Feel partner always wins conflicts
19. Accept conflict as inevitable in marriage
20. Believe we fight too much

2. Now go back over the statements again and place an *0* by the number you believe is true of the way your partner handles disagreements.

3. Go through the list together. Try not to get defensive. Remember, defensiveness is a barrier to communication. By sharing your perceptions of your own and your partner's typical behaviors, you may gain a better understanding of how you relate to each other when disagreements and conflict arise. Be careful to use good speaking-for-self statements like, "I believe that is often true for me when I'm angry with you," or, "I think this is often what you do when you are angry with me."

Are you satisfied with the ways you usually behave when confronted with conflict and anger? Does this dialogue suggest some ways you would like to change? If so, note the changes you think might be helpful. We hope after reading this chapter you will have some additional ideas that will help you contain anger and resolve conflicts.

WHAT THE BIBLE SAYS
ABOUT ANGER

The Bible is full of references to anger, and provides significant insights into the nature of anger and how Christians
should deal with it. Many of the references to anger in the
Scripture refer to God as being angry. In the New Testament,
we read of Jesus being angry with the merchants and money
changers who were desecrating the temple (John 2:13-17),
and at another time with the Pharisees (Mark 3:5). Jesus, in
the Sermon on the Mount, accepts the fact that people do
get angry (Matt. 5:21-26) as does Paul when he writes to the
Ephesians, "Be angry, and sin not" (4:26).

The Bible teaches that anger is a natural, normal, inevitable emotion. Anger as an emotion is a part of God's creative
genius and fulfills a vital purpose in our lives. The feeling of

anger is a warning that something is wrong. It prepares us physically to run or to fight. The next time you are angry, notice how much energy you have. This energy is, in fact, what makes anger dangerous.

Is it, then, a sin to be angry? We do not think so. In fact, we believe it is impossible not to get angry. Anger as a pure emotion is simply a part of our creation. We can no more keep from feeling it than we can fear or embarrassment. The sin is not in the feeling of anger, but in the way we behave in response to the feeling. Feelings are just feelings and not open to judgment.

Jesus, in the Sermon on the Mount, while accepting the inevitability of anger, also clearly recognized it as a dangerous emotion. It holds within it the seeds of violent and destructive behavior. To avoid this behavior, He taught that anger must be dealt with in its initial stage:

> If therefore you are presenting your offering at the altar, and there remember that your brother has something against you, leave your offering there before the altar, and go your way; first be reconciled to your brother, and then come and present your offering.
>
> (Matt. 5:23-25, NASB)

Jesus cautioned us to recognize and accept our anger quickly to avoid letting it become hostility, revenge, spite or violence. Even if you are about a task as important as worship and realize that you are angry at your brother or wife, go and immediately deal with the anger. Jesus knew that anger is easiest to deal with in its initial stage. The longer you hold on to the anger, the more it swells. And the more it swells, the more difficult it is to control the behavior anger can spawn.

Anger, then, is a warning to closely monitor our feelings and our behavior. While marriage and family life provide an overabundance of opportunities for anger to get out of hand, the Scripture is clear on our responsibilities to handle our anger in a loving, caring way. The husband and wife who want to love each other as Christ loved the church will learn to identify their anger in the early stages and work through that anger with their partner in a way that respects the Christ image in each other.

Finally, the Bible teaches us to be quick to forgive. The concept of forgiveness is central to the Christian faith. Forgiveness comes from God, but it carries with it a requirement. "And forgive us our debts as we also have forgiven our debtors" (Matt. 6:12, NASB). This is the only petition in the model prayer of Jesus that has to do with human relationships. All the rest are free gifts to us from God. But if we are to be free from the burden of guilt, then we must be forgiving in our relationships with our neighbors (see also Matt. 18:23-27). We believe that this is particularly true when dealing with our closest neighbor—our spouse.

The Bible speaks throughout to the complexities of human relationships. And the theme is always the same: sin, repentance, and forgiveness; anger, separation, and reconciliation. When all wisdom, logic, and rationality fail, forgiveness alone may be the salvation of the relationship.

THE NATURE OF MARITAL CONFLICT

Susie and David have been married almost a year. They married out of a strong desire for warmth, closeness, and companionship. Lately, however, their disagreements have led to increased conflict and a feeling of distance. Anger is more pervasive in their interaction, and they fear their love may be slipping away from them.

Susie and David are caught in what David Mace, in his book *Love and Anger in Marriage,* calls the "love-anger cycle." As they move closer to each other in search of intimacy, they become more aware of their differences. Differences that earlier may have seemed attractive or at least unimportant become threatening and move them into disagreement. Now they have a problem. If they move away from each other, they lose the intimacy they seek; but if they move closer together, their disagreement heats up and becomes conflict. The conflict stirs up feelings of irritation, resentment, hostility, and disillusionment.

At this point many couples retreat to a position of distance and, at least temporarily, give up the search for intimacy. Dr. Mace's point is that we seek intimacy to receive love. As we do, the inevitable differences between us become disagreements and heat up into conflict. This releases a flood of anger which threatens love. Shocked and hurt, we back away and abandon the quest for intimacy. A couple may repeat this process many times, caught in the deadly love-anger cycle.

"Is there no other way?" you may be asking. "Can't the love-anger cycle be broken? Must a couple give up forever the push for closeness?" Fortunately, couples can learn to deal with both the conflict their differences produce and the anger resulting from it. The solution requires accepting anger as a healthy emotion and understanding it as an ally of the relationship. It is then possible to use good communication skills to help your partner understand your anger and to help negotiate a resolution to the conflict. What this means in terms of the love-anger cycle is that a couple must be willing to tolerate the heat and discomfort of their anger and push on toward their goal of intimacy. Running from the discomfort of anger can only mean distancing yourself from your partner.

THE CREATIVE USE OF CONFLICT IN MARRIAGE

Is it possible? Can conflict be a source of creative growth for a marriage? The early years of our marriage would have refuted that idea. In the last ten years, however, we have learned that, when handled appropriately, conflict can be a gift to the relationship that opens doors and windows to new possibilities and opportunities for growth. It has not been easy. We have both had to change our typical approaches to anger and conflict—stuffing and yelling. Two new skills helped us. The first was learning how to contain the anger that conflict generates. The second was negotiating the differences out of which the conflict arose.

Containing the Anger

Before we talk more about anger, we would like for you to do an exercise to help you learn more about anger in your relationship. You will be using some of the skills in developing self-awareness that you learned in Chapter 3.

Exercise N: Using the Awareness Wheel to Understand Anger

1. Read through the following questions making some notes to yourself in preparation for discussing them with your partner.

   Sensations: What typical situations cause you to feel angry toward your spouse? What kinds of things do you see, hear, or otherwise perceive that cause you to feel angry?

   Thinking: What are some of your beliefs about anger? Is it natural? Is it inevitable? What do you think about your own anger? Do you have a temper? Can you control it? Do you think you get angry too often? Not often enough?

Feelings: What other feelings accompany your anger? Thinking about some of your sensations above, what are some feelings you have in addition to or prior to the anger? Anger is a secondary emotion; that is, it usually follows another primary emotion such as hurt, frustration, embarrassment, or guilt. Often, if you can identify the underlying primary emotions, it is easier to deal with the secondary emotion, anger.

Actions: How do you act when you feel angry? How do you act when you become aware of your partner's anger?

Intentions: How would you like to deal with your anger? How would you like your spouse to deal with his/her anger? How would you like to deal with your anger in relation to each other?

2. When you and your partner are both ready, discuss your answers with each other. Rather than one of you going through all five parts of the awareness wheel, take each section of the awareness wheel and both discuss it before moving to the next section. If you decide that you want to make some changes, we hope the suggestions on the next few pages will be helpful.

In our first marriage enrichment training experience, David and Vera Mace taught us a three-step process for dealing with anger. These three steps follow closely the biblical principles we identified earlier. The process seems simple but is harder to put into effect than to talk about. It was worth the effort, however, because ultimately it changed the way we related to each other. The three steps as we use them are: (1) communicate the anger, (2) disarm the anger, and (3) process the anger. The process requires that both partners agree to follow the steps.

Step 1: Communicate the anger

Just saying, "I am angry with you," sounds simple, doesn't it? In practice, you may find it much more difficult. For Preston, simply saying it instead of shouting it was the difficult part. He wanted to show how angry he was rather than just announcing it. For Genie, who had always believed that anger was destructive to relationships, openly saying the words was frightening.

Notice the "speaking-for-self" skill in communicating the anger. The typical way of communicating anger is to say, "You make me so mad." As you learned in Chapter 3, a "you" statement puts the blame on the hearer. "You are responsible for my anger." Probably your anger is the result of something you think your partner has done, but the angry feeling is yours. You are the one who is angry, and your anger is based on how you perceive the situation. We are not saying that you make yourself angry. However, the anger belongs to you, and communicating through an "I" statement may prevent your partner from becoming defensive. We have found communicating the anger much easier if we follow the scriptural instruction to acknowledge the anger soon after we become aware of it—that is, while it is only a "pinch." The longer we wait, the more likely Preston is to be a yeller and Genie to be a stuffer.

Step 2: Disarm the anger

The second step is to dissolve or disarm the anger so that it does not push you apart. Most people deal with anger primarily in one of two ways. Some *suppress* their anger— stuffing it down inside, pretending that it is not there. This was Genie's typical way of handling her anger. She did it so quickly that sometimes she was not even aware of it. Suppressed anger frequently comes out in unwanted ways like ulcers, heart attacks, and accidents. Sometimes it appears indirectly in behavior such as being late, being sexually unresponsive, not recording checks, an so on. At other times it finally erupts in violent outbursts. It is generally agreed that habitually suppressing anger is not good for individuals or relationships.

Other people *vent* their anger. Sometimes this is done in healthy ways such as jogging or housecleaning—making use of the tremendous energy anger produces. Often this is a good first step to getting the anger in control. It drains off some of the energy. It is not so good, however, if the energy is drained off indirectly and never used to deal with the problem out of which the anger comes.

Other people take a more direct route. They vent their anger through verbal and sometimes physical attacks. Preston's yelling was this kind of venting. Venting anger is reinforced by the personal cleansing it seems to bring. Preston's angry outbursts lasted only a few minutes. Afterwards, he felt wonderful and was ready to move immediately back into the relationship—to go out to dinner, make love, whatever. From a purely individual standpoint, this kind of venting is very satisfying; but we are now convinced that it is disastrous for relationships. While Preston felt good, relieved of the anger, Genie was left with her fear and anger from having been attacked. Because she did not vent her anger in the same way, these feelings lasted much longer for her and resulted in a temporary loss of relationship.

We were both frustrated with the way we typically handled our anger until David Mace introduced us to a third way—an alternative to either suppressing or venting anger. We learned that rather than choosing to suppress the anger or to vent the anger, we could choose to *dissolve* the anger. Preston prefers to use the term "disarm" rather than "dissolve" since he finds that sometimes the emotion lingers, but at such a decreased intensity that he does not want to attack.

You probably know more about dissolving anger than you think. Imagine yourself in a crowded place. The crowd is pressing around you. Suddenly, the person in front of you steps back on your toe. Feel the pain. You shake it off. But before the pain is entirely gone he steps back again. Now the toe really hurts. You feel your anger begin to rise. You think, *What is wrong with this guy? Why can't he stay off my foot?* Then the crowd shifts, and he does it a third time right on the same toe. *He is doing it on purpose; he wants to hurt me,* you think, and your anger swells. Just then the man turns slightly. As he does you see—he is totally blind!

What happened to your anger? Is it gone—dissolved? Or perhaps it is not gone but has greatly receded—disarmed. Why did it change? Maybe because you replaced one thought with another. Rather than thinking, *He is out to get me,* you think, *Oh, he is blind. In this crowd it is hard for him to keep his balance. He wasn't really out to hurt me.* The feeling is changed by changing the thought.

In marital conflict, when you first feel the anger, the thought is often, *S/he's out to get me; s/he's taking advantage of me; s/he wants to hurt me.* The anger is our natural defense to such a perceived attack. To dissolve the anger we need to replace that thought with another. As soon as he felt like shouting at Genie, Preston learned to think instead, *Hey, wait a minute. This is Genie—my lover, my friend, my wife. She's really not out to get me. She is not my enemy. It's not appropriate to attack her with my anger.*

If you are going to use this step, it is absolutely essential that you contract to never again attack each other with your anger. It was obvious how Preston was attacking Genie—by shouting. But it was less obvious how she attacked him. We finally realized that her withdrawal, her not talking, her

distancing herself, was really just as much of an attack as Preston's yelling. So you may have to figure out how each is attacking the other. It may be silence, withdrawal of affection, or some other indirect way instead of the easily recognized, direct onslaughts. Whatever form the attack takes, the contract is to never again use it as a means of handling anger. Once secure with this contract, it is much easier to take the measures necessary to disarm the anger so that you can move on to step three.

Step 3: Process the anger

What we mean by processing the anger is sitting down together; discussing the situation out of which the anger developed; and trying to understand the thoughts, feelings, and wants behind the anger. In step two you rid yourself of the anger or at least disarm it so that it is under control. The temptation at this point is to say, "Let's forget it. Let's not risk a blowup." But if you stop there, the same situation is likely to occur again. And the more often that situation arises, the more difficult it is to keep control of your anger.

Instead of dropping it, I need to ask my partner for help. "I'm angry with you, but I don't want to stay angry with you. I won't attack you with my anger. But I do need your help. I want to resolve this situation so I won't keep getting angry about it." If you can say this in a nonblaming style of communication, there is a good chance your partner will appreciate the invitation to help resolve the situation. After all, s/he has a stake in working out the problem, avoiding the anger, and maintaining the relationship. The more often you follow through with this step, the more trust you gain in the contract you made in step two, as well as in your overall ability to handle your own and your partner's anger.

Negotiating Differences

As you process the situation in step three, you may discover that you still have conflicting differences. Some means of resolving the differences must be found. Joe wants to buy a new car, but Joan is opposed to accumulating more debt at the time. She is considering going back to school and wants to leave open the option of quitting her job. What do they do?

Joe and Joan can choose one of three types of negotiation—compromise, accommodation, or what we call the "love gift." Of these three, *compromise* is probably the best known. It requires that both partners process their differences until they find a point at which both can be comfortable. Sometimes this means finding a third alternative— something different from where either began. At other times it means each gets only a part of what s/he wants. And at other times it may mean that Joan will go along with Joe on one decision if Joe will go along with her on another. The nature of compromise, however, is that neither will get exactly what he wants.

The second means of dealing with difference is through *accommodation* or coexistence. Accommodation simply means agreeing to disagree. At all levels of human relationships, accommodation is a process that people use for living together. "We cannot agree on this at this time, but we respect each other's position and agree to disagree on it." Our experience over twenty-seven years of marriage is that areas of accommodation change over time. Differences of opinion that seemed so enormous to us at earlier times have now disappeared, or we have found other ways around them. But we still have some areas in which we disagree. We acknowledge we cannot agree but are willing to live with it. While every relationship probably has some areas of accommodation, most cannot tolerate too many. An excess of accommodation will eventually take its toll.

David Mace calls the third form of negotiation "capitulation." To us the word *capitulation* has a negative connotation—something like giving in or losing. That is clearly not what we or Mace mean. We have, therefore, renamed this form of negotiation the "love gift."

All forms of negotiation require good communication skills, yet the third is far more dependent on communication which leads to understanding than the other two. The love gift occurs when both parties have discussed the issue until one, out of his understanding, is able to say, "Now I understand why you think and feel the way you do about this and why it is so important to you. I have not really changed how I see it; but because I understand its importance to you, I'm willing to go along with you on it." Now that's not giving in. That's not losing. That's the love gift.

The love gift can come only out of understanding. If I give in too quickly because of reluctance to thoroughly process the conflict, it is avoidance. If I give in and go along with you because I feel overpowered, it is dominance. If I demand the love gift because I gave in the last time, it is competition. If I do not feel good in the giving, it is not the love gift. The gift comes totally out of my understanding and love for you. The feeling is something like the one you have when you have been able to choose a gift for someone whom you truly adore. It is the fulfillment of Jesus' words, "It is more blessed to give than to receive" (Acts 20:35, NIV).

The love gift is not always the most appropriate form of negotiation to choose. If one partner cannot sincerely give it, the couple needs to use either accommodation or compromise. At times in our life together, we would have made a serious mistake had either of us given the love gift. Fortunately, we each continued to hold to and discuss our positions until a third possibility emerged that was ultimately better for us than either of our original stands. The love gift has the greatest potential for relationship building, but the other two forms of negotiation are important, too. All three provide a means for using conflict as a source of creative growth in marriage.

To summarize and apply what you have learned in this chapter, we would like for you to do the following exercise. The exercise is based on the use of communication skills, so you may want to review what you learned in Chapters 3 and 4.

Exercise O: Resolving Conflict

1. On separate sheets of paper, each partner list all of the areas of conflict currently under negotiation in your relationship.
2. When you have finished, discuss your lists and select one issue on which you both would be willing to work. Choose one of midrange intensity to practice rather than choosing the most difficult one or one that neither of you has strong feelings about. Once you have agreed on the issue, follow these steps in processing the conflict.

   a. Set a time and place for discussion, including a time to end. Even if you are not through by that time, stop and make an appointment to resume at another time.

   b. Define the problem or issue of disagreement. Each write out the partner's position—what s/he wants, thinks, feels—and then exchange papers. If your partner has not worded your position accurately, you rewrite it and exchange papers again. You may eventually skip the writing and give verbal feedback.

   c. How do you contribute to the problem? Without blaming, using "I" statements, discuss what each of you does to block solutions to the problem.

   d. List things you have done in the past which have not been successful.

   e. Brainstorm and list all possible solutions. This is a creative dreaming process. Try not to be bound by realities such as time and money. You can eliminate the totally unrealistic ones in the next step.

f. Thoroughly discuss each of these solutions, being sure to consider each other as you evaluate each possibility.

g. Agree on one solution to try.

h. Contract with each other on the specific ways you will work to achieve the solution.

i. Make an appointment for another time to discuss your progress. If something is not working, adjust your contract.

j. Be aware of your partner's efforts toward the solution and affirm those efforts with both words and deeds.

Using this ten-step approach to conflict negotiation may seem cumbersome in the beginning. The more you use it, however, the more comfortable you will become with it. As you have some success with it, you will also gain more confidence in your ability to resolve your differences as a couple. You may even discover that this new confidence creates a new kind of intimacy, one that grows out of your ability to use conflict creatively in your relationship.

Chapter Six

USING COMMUNICATION SKILLS TO GROW IN ONENESS

*T*HE BIBLICAL CONCEPT of oneness refers to sharing our spiritual, emotional, and physical selves in the marital relationship. David and Vera Mace in their book *Marriage Enrichment in the Church* ask,

> What is the heart of the Christian experience? Isn't it to know that you are loved and accepted by God and that you are, therefore, a worthwhile person? And if this spiritual experience can be matched by a marriage in which you are fully known, and deeply loved, by the one person with whom you share life day by day, then surely your cup runs over![1]

It is the desire for oneness or intimacy that draws most couples into marriage. The impersonality of contemporary society

---

[1]David and Vera Mace, *Marriage Enrichment in the Church,* (Nashville: Broadman, 1976), p. 21.

stimulates a need to escape into the openness, unity, and closeness of an intimate relationship. Consequently, creating intimacy is a goal for most couples.

CREATING INTIMACY

What does intimacy mean to you? Some of the words that come to our minds are closeness, vulnerability, oneness, trust. You can probably think of many more. Use the following exercise to explore what intimacy means to each of you.

Exercise P: What Is Intimacy?

1. Make a list of all the words that come to mind when you think of intimacy.
2. When you both have completed your lists, talk about the various meanings you associate with intimacy.
3. Talk together now about how each of you experiences intimacy in your relationship. How satisfied are you with the current level of intimacy? Try to talk about this objectively and avoid blame. The next exercise will give you some ideas about how to increase the level of intimacy.

When the word *intimacy* is used, many people think only of sexual or physical intimacy. Actually there are many kinds of intimacy: spiritual, emotional, intellectual, aesthetic, crisis. But none of these just happen.

Often when you feel an absence of intimacy in your relationship, the easiest thing to do is to blame your partner for the loss. We frequently have couples come to us for counseling with one partner saying, "I'm not sure I love my wife/

husband anymore." What this person is saying most often is that s/he has lost the feelings of closeness, being connected, excitement, that we call intimacy. Most are surprised when we ask, "What have you done to create intimacy?" "Create intimacy? Do you mean there is something that I can do to make my relationship more intimate?" Many of these couples, once they accept the fact that the level of intimacy in their marriage is in their hands, are eager to learn ways to create more intimacy. In this chapter we want to talk about some ways you can use effective communication to create intimacy or oneness in your marriage.

Encouraging Openness

Intimacy most often occurs when two people are able to lower their defenses, become vulnerable, and share with each other their emotions, thoughts, and desires. When we are willing to be open and vulnerable, a feeling of intimacy and closeness develops. When one person is willing to tell another his deepest awareness, a bond develops and makes the other more willing to share her awareness. For this to occur there must be trust—trust that neither partner will be put down because of what has been revealed, trust that what has been revealed will not be used to gain an advantage or shared outside the relationship. This level of trust produces an atmosphere of openness that encourages people to share their lives in a way that draws them into a more intimate relationship.

Communication that verbally and nonverbally conveys the message that I care about you, about myself, and about our relationship helps to create an atmosphere of openness. Miller, Nunnally, and Wackman in *Talking Together* suggest that in couple relationships all communication must include an "I count you/I count me" message. The goal is to make decisions and act on ideas in such a manner that both partners feel understood and valued. To communicate from this position requires using all the skills we have learned. I count myself when I explore my awareness and am willing to share appropriate parts with my partner. I count you when I am a good listener and encourage you to share your awareness with me. I discount myself when I withhold important thoughts and feelings from you. I discount you when I say, "You couldn't possibly think that," or, "You shouldn't feel that way." Communicating from an "I count you/I count me" position sets the stage for intimacy.

Suggestions for Increasing Intimacy
Certainly couples cannot expect constantly to have feelings of deepest intimacy, but neither can they sit back and wait for closeness to happen spontaneously. Some of the best ideas for creating intimacy may come from your own marital experience. The following exercise might help you identify ways to increase closeness.

Exercise Q: Creating Intimacy
1. Think of three times when you felt particularly close to your partner.
2. Share these with your spouse.
3. Now think about what happened to allow those intimate feelings to occur.
4. Talk about those with your partner.

One of the first factors most couples identify in this exercise is having unhurried time together. We talked about this at length in Chapter 2. It is difficult to feel close to someone when you have little time to be together. Schedule some time together to talk about your day; some time to relax together; and some time to share your deeper thoughts, feelings, and concerns about your life together.

Showing appreciation and caring for each other is another means of creating intimacy. When you feel your partner ap-

preciates you for just being you and for what you contribute to the relationship, feelings of closeness naturally develop. Couples sometimes find it easier to talk about the negatives than the positives—both in their relationship and in their partner. Think of a positive thought you have had about your partner lately. Perhaps you felt proud of the way s/he handled a job outside the home or you appreciated her taking care of a routine duty at home. Did you tell her that you felt good about that? Try overdosing with compliments or affirming statements. It is sure to help build intimacy. Practice saying thank you, or "I liked the way you did that," and try eliminating some of the negative statements.

Demonstrating "I care about you" is another sure way to increase intimacy. We are not talking about big things. Small, thoughtful gestures can have a major impact. But first you must be sure what says "I care" to your partner. Your ideas and hers might not be the same. This is a good place to practice your request-making skills.

Exercise R: Demonstrating Caring

1. List on a sheet of paper five to ten behaviors you would like to receive from your partner that say "I care" or "I appreciate you." These should be simple, positive, specific. For instance: "I would like for you to bring me a cup of coffee when I wake up in the morning." "I would like for you to give me ten minutes to relax when I come home in the evening." "Bring me a two-dollar surprise." "Cuddle with me for five minutes before we go to sleep."

2. Share your list with your partner and be sure each knows what the other is requesting.

3. Now agree to do at least two items from your partner's list per day for the next week. Your agreement should be that you will carry out your part whether or not your partner does.

4. Each night take a few minutes to see if each of you received your two "I cares." Sometimes they are sent but not recognized. Be sure to show your appreciation to your partner by affirming his/her actions each day.

Sharing goals and interests is another way to create intimacy. You don't have to share all your partner's interests, but you need some in common. You can show interest in those you do not share by listening to your partner when s/he tells you about what s/he experiences and from time to time going along. Talking about goals, both personal and relational, brings partners closer to each other. When you talk together about your dreams and share common goals and values, a bond is built that outlasts the conversation.

Celebrating Differences

One of the great mysteries of marriage is how two people can become one and yet remain two. Marriage is not the blending of two personalities into one, but the joining of two unique individuals into one relationship. Contemporary marriages require the strength of two whole people quite capable of standing on their own. When these unique persons freely join in relationship, the whole becomes greater than the sum of its parts. The relationship becomes a part of and adds to their individual strengths. The ancient writers described this quality of marriage as being like a rope of great strength because it is made up of three strands.

The unity candle in the wedding ceremony beautifully symbolizes this element of marriage. Three candles stand unlighted in a candelabra. The parents of the bride and the parents of the groom light the candles on either side. These candles represent the individuality of the bride and the groom, and the uniqueness of each one's life experiences. They are lighted by the parents to symbolize the heritage each brings from his or her family. After they have exchanged vows, the couple together comes to the unity candle. Each takes the candle lighted by his or her parents and simultaneously lights the center candle. This candle represents their relationship—their oneness in God. In some traditions the bride and groom then blow out their own candles leaving only the center candle burning. We prefer the symbolism of replacing the still burning tapers in the holder. The three brightly burning candles represent the unique personhood each partner brings to the marriage plus the covenant relationship they have established. Marriage takes nothing away from either individual; it actually enhances each partner.

As beautiful as the symbolism is, the actual process is more difficult. Often your differences get in the way of the intimacy you seek. Growing individually while growing in oneness is something partners must work at throughout their marriage. Each partner has a need to be his own, independent person but also needs to experience the intimacy of relationship. Marriage gains strength from the unique contributions of each partner but each partner must also be willing to give up a portion of independence to create the interdependence necessary for an intimate relationship to develop. The differences each of us brings to the marriage present both pleasures and challenges.

You can use the communication skills you have learned to express your appreciation for the unique contributions your partner brings to your marriage. Remember, to be most effective, statements of appreciation should be very specific: "I really appreciate the way you worked out the details for our trip. I really hate doing that," rather than, "You are so good at details." When challenges occur, rely on good listening skills to convey acceptance, "I" statements to avoid conveying judgment, self-disclosure statements to increase understanding, and request-making skills to initiate change. Use the following exercise to practice these skills.

Exercise S: Affirming Differences

1. Think about the differences (uniqueness) that you and your partner have. Each of you make a list.
2. Now note how the differences you listed contribute positively to your marriage. For example, Preston believes money is security. He wants to save as much as possible for a rainy day. On the other hand, Genie thinks money is to be enjoyed and is not very concerned about saving. This has had a positive influence on our relationship in that Preston has learned from Genie to enjoy spending money on extras, and Genie has learned to be more intentional in saving. Our differences have helped us achieve a balance in this area.
3. After you have completed your lists, share them with each other. Remember to focus on the positives and to use the communication skills you have learned.

INTENTIONAL MARRIAGE

When we married, our goal was to have a really good marriage. On the day of our wedding we had the potential to achieve that goal. Unfortunately, we did not know how to maximize that potential. So for fourteen years we settled for less than the warm, tender, loving, creative relationship we had envisioned. We had an okay marriage.

Having an okay marriage did not take much effort for us. Then, as we described in the Introduction, we were faced with a challenge. Out of that situation we discovered that it was our responsibility to make our relationship what we wanted it to be. God had given us the potential, the resources, to have a good marriage. Until that point we had not been good stewards of those precious resources. When we began to take responsibility for making our relationship what we wanted it to be, we found a potential for fulfillment that we had not experienced previously. Through our commitment to each other to intentionally work to develop that potential, we experienced a deepening of love, trust, mutual understanding, and support of each other.

We often ask couples in our programs, "What has marriage enrichment done for your marriage?" The most frequent answer is, "We have discovered that our marriage does not have to go its own way. We can maintain some control and not just react to whatever happens to us as individuals, as a couple, or in the world outside our relationship." Many of these couples report that the greatest benefit they have received is the confidence of knowing they can make plans for their relationship and work together toward achieving goals they have established. "We can influence the direction of our relationship. Together we can work toward greater fulfillment and satisfaction by setting goals and working toward attaining those goals. We decide how we want our relationship to develop and use our skills and knowledge to help us grow in those directions."

What these couples are describing is what we call "intentional marriage." Marital relationships continually change. A couple can help to determine the direction of that change by being intentional. To be intentional means to decide together what you want from your relationship, to set goals, and to contract with each other for specific ways (behavior changes) you will seek to attain those goals. Each time we sit down with a group of couples in a marriage enrichment event, our primary objective is to help them become more intentional about their relationships. We have discovered that the only way to be intentional about marriage is to actively plan for relationship growth. So we always end our

events by helping couples develop growth plans for their marriages. We would like to end our time with you in the same way by encouraging you to develop a growth plan for your marriage.

Marital Growth Plan
Many people set goals for business, church, children, clubs or organizations. And yet how many consider setting goals for their marriage relationship? We have had many growth plans throughout the last twelve years of our marriage. In fact we always have a current plan for our relationship. As an example here is one of our contracts:

MARITAL GROWTH CONTRACT

Date

Goal 1: To be more intentional about creating intimacy.
1. Both of us will strive to express positive feelings and our appreciation of each other more often.
2. Genie will work at expressing her irritations earlier so they will not block intimacy. Preston will be slower about expressing negative feelings, considering whether they are really important.
3. We will spend the first hour after we both get home in the evening talking with each other about our day. We will avoid dealing with any negative relationship issues during this time.
4. On Sunday night we will designate one night that week neither of us will work. Each will take responsibility for creating a loving atmosphere and planning things we both enjoy doing.

Goal 2: To reduce anxiety and guilt about outside tasks.
  1. Genie will make and update the list of what needs to be done, and on Monday evenings we will agree on assignments.
  2. Preston will move faster to get things done or at least give Genie a time by which it will be done.
  3. Genie won't "bug" Preston about his assignments as long as they are done by the agreed time.

Goal 3: To be more consistent in using our communication skills.
  1. Preston will be quicker to share what he is thinking with Genie.
  2. Genie will work at identifying her feelings earlier and sharing them.
  3. We will both be more careful about using "I" statements.
  4. We will affirm each other for making the effort to use the skills.

We have found contracts like this one to be extremely helpful in keeping us focused on the areas in which we are seeking to develop our potential. Here is how we go about it.

Exercise T: Planning for Growth

  1. Looking back at the exercises you have completed throughout this study, we would like for you, as a couple, to identify three goals that you would like to work toward for the next three months. For example, you might have a goal in relation to how you communicate, how you handle conflict, or how to create intimacy in your relationship. Work on this together and come to an agreement on the three goals. We strongly suggest using only three goals.
  2. Now take the first goal and under it list the behaviors each of you *is willing* to practice to help you reach that

goal. If your goal is to communicate more on a regular basis, you might say, "Jean will arrange her schedule in the evenings so we can have twenty minutes after dinner to catch up on each other's day. Tom will arrange an evening every two weeks for us to have an evening alone to talk about our relationship. Jean and Tom will use the awareness wheel individually to become self-aware of issues and then share that awareness with the other." These are your contracts. Make your contracts simple, positive, and direct. Be sure when you make the contract that it is something you are willing to do. Do not make a contract you know will not do. After you have made contracts for the first goal move to the second and third.

A few words about the future of your contracts and goals. First, keep your growth plan in a place where you both will see it at least daily and preferably several times a day—the mirror in your bathroom or bedroom, on the closet door, or on the refrigerator door. The idea is to place it where you will see it often, and it will call your attention to the agreements you have made.

Next, set a time aside *each week* to sit down together and talk about your goals and contracts. Are you making progress? Are the contracts you made moving you toward your goal? Are each of you fulfilling your contracts? If the answers to these questions are "yes," celebrate your progress! If you must repeatedly answer "no," decide how you can change your contracts to make them work for you.

Don't give up too quickly on a contract. Give yourselves a chance to make it work. But don't keep items in your contract that you have not been able or willing to do for several weeks. If you find you have a contract that hasn't worked after three or four weeks, renegotiate the contract inserting different behaviors that you are more likely to do it. It is depressing to have a contract that doesn't work. The objective of the contracts is to produce growth, and if they are not doing that, then you need new ones. Remember, behavior changes slowly. We have found that most often when contracts do not work, it is because we are trying to change too much too fast. Behavior change is more likely to occur when you work in small increments.

At the end of three months look together at where you were when you began and where you are now. Decide if you have accomplished your goals. Then either make new goals and contracts or refine some of the ones you already have. This can be a continuous process that through the years will help you remain intentional in your relationship growth.

In Chapter 1 we emphasized covenant as being the undergirding force in God's plan for marriage. The concept of contracting for relationship growth brings us back to where we began. The strength of marriage between Christians lies in the covenant that they make between themselves and individually with God. Contracting for relationship growth recognizes the dynamic or ever-changing quality of human relationships and God's redeeming presence in those relationships. Legal contracts can fail because of their rigid, tit-for-tat nature. If one party does not live up to the terms of the agreement, it is invalid. But the covenant relationship is not just between two individuals. God's presence in the covenant reinforces the commitment of each partner to work for the good of the relationship regardless of the other partner's participation in whatever contracts they establish with each other. When two Christians, seeking God's purpose for their marriage, identify goals for growth and contract with each other to achieve those goals, they are actualizing the concept of covenant marriage. God has become a part of their plan. Their contract has the additional element of covenant.

May you feel God's blessings and His guidance as you work together for an enriched marriage.

SUGGESTED READING

Broderick, Carlfred. *Couples.* New York: Touchstone Books, 1981.

Herring, Reuben; Hester, Jimmy; & Jordan, Ken, compilers. *Models for Marriage Enrichment in the Church.* Nashville: Baptist Sunday School Board, 1988.

Howell, John. *Equality and Submission in Marriage.* Nashville: Broadman Press, 1979.

Liontos, Lynn & Liontos, Demetri. *The Good Couple Life.* Winston-Salem: Association for Couples in Marriage Enrichment, 1985.

Mace, David. *Love and Anger in Marriage.* Grand Rapids: Zondervan, 1982.

Mace, David & Mace, Vera. *How to Have a Happy Marriage.* Nashville: Abingdon, 1983.

Mace, David, & Mace, Vera. *Marriage Enrichment in the Church.* Nashville: Broadman Press, 1976.

Miller, Sherod; Nunnally, Elam; & Wackman, Daniel B. *Talking Together.* Minneapolis: Interpersonal Communication Programs, Inc., 1979.

Penner, Clifford & Penner, Joyce. *The Gift of Sex.* Waco: Word Books, 1981.

Stuart, Richard. *Helping Couples Change.* New York: Guilford Press, 1980.

Stuart, Richard & Jacobson, Barbara. *Second Marriage.* New York: W.W. Norton, Co., Inc., 1985.

TEACHING PROCEDURES

The Process

We have used the same process to write this book that we use in our marriage enrichment events. We suggest you use it as you teach *The Language of Married Love.* The process flows as follows:

Connecting: Building closeness with self, partner, and group

Assessing: Taking an honest look at where your marriage is today; that is, creating a desire for growth

Learning: Identifying needed knowledge and skills

Planning: Contracting for intentional growth using new knowledge and skills

Keep this process in mind as you plan from the first session to the last and for each session.

Couples learn best by doing. Therefore, we have included exercises throughout the book. Encourage participants to read the book and do the exercises before group sessions. If you are doing this on a weekend schedule or consecutive-night schedule, have them read the book and do the exercises before the first session. Ask participants to bring their exercises to the sessions. Rely heavily on exercises and limit lecturettes to ten minutes.

Couple dialogue is the primary method. The only way a couple will improve communication is by talking together. Exercises provide a structured way to do that. Partners are encouraged to talk to each other and then to other couples. Couples can learn much from one another if they share experiences in a helping way. To create this kind of sharing, use the following ground rules.

1. All sharing is voluntary.
2. Share *experiences:* do not analyze, diagnose, or give advice.
3. What is shared in the group is confidential.

The best way to encourage participants to dialogue and share couple to couple is for the leader couple or facilitator to model an exercise. Be sure that you model good communication skills. Do not let general group discussion take time away from individual couple dialogue time. Remember that for some couples this will be the first and only time they spend seriously talking with each other.

Structure

Couples learn best in small groups. Select a room that is comfortable and has movable chairs. Up to eight couples can work well as one group. If you have more than eight, divide them into groups of three couples. Keep the same groups throughout the sessions. You can lead from the front and allow them to interact in the small groups. You may feel somewhat out of control with this format, but trust the group process.

The material is designed for six, one-and-one-half- to two-hour sessions. Adjust the material accordingly for other formats.

Session 1: Marriage and the Importance of Communication

Connecting: Invite participants to experience a memory journey. Ask them to close their eyes and imagine a large book like a family Bible. It is the book of their relationship. Ask them to turn to the first page. Have them slowly flip through the pages as you ask them to remember:

1. The very first time they saw their partners. What was s/he wearing?

What were your thoughts and feelings?

2. The first date they had—where they went, what they did and again thoughts or feelings.
3. The time at which they knew they were in love and wanted to spend the rest of their lives together.
4. Their wedding, particularly the service and becoming aware of each other as husband and wife.
5. The first place they lived together. Have them walk through the different rooms remembering times, thoughts, and feelings they shared.
6. Finally ask them to quickly flip through the rest of the book remembering some high points of their marriage—children, vacations, new home, and so on.

Ask them to slowly come back to the present, open their eyes and, when they are ready, share their memory journey with their spouse.

Break into groups of three couples if needed. Ask couples to take turns answering the following questions in their group: what are your names; how did you meet; how long have you been married; who makes up your family; what is unique about your relationship?

Assessing: Read Genesis 1 and 2 to the group and have them do Exercise A: Marital Expectations (Chapter 1, page 12). After they have shared as a couple, have them make a combined list of expectations for their group. If you have several groups, ask each to contribute to a general list. Relate the expectations on the list to God's purpose of companionship.

Learning: Ask, "What makes it hard to create a relationship based on companionship?" Use their responses to lead into a lecturette on covenant marriage emphasizing the six dimensions. Ask each person to think about how each of these dimensions works in his marriage. Have them share their evaluations with their partner. Finally focus on the importance of communication to develop and maintain a relationship based on the six dimensions.

Planning: Have couples do Exercise B: What Do We Talk About? (Chapter 1, page 20). Have them select at least one topic from the second list to work on during the week. Also have them agree on specific times during the next week they will read the text and do the exercises.

Session 2: Barriers and Bridges

Connecting: Divide participants into groups of no more than eight each with spouses in separate groups. Ask them to identify any fears they might have for participating in this study. Have someone make a list. Now have them discuss and list what they hope to achieve through this study. Have each group read its lists for the benefit of the other groups.

Have spouses sit together and identify and share privately their own fears and hopes. Ask if anyone has any concerns generated out of the last session of their work during the week. Do not fix concerns; just be empathetic and create hope.

Assessing: Ask couples to look at the list of barriers and bridges they made from Exercise D in Chapter 2 (page 33). Do they need to add anything to either list? In their small groups ask them to share first from their list of barriers. They need not share everything on the list. Compile a group list. Make a master list by asking each group to contribute three or four barriers mentioned in their group until all identified items have been put on the list once. Don't discuss the items; just list them.

Repeat the above procedure to identify bridges. Emphasize the concept of tearing down the barriers and using those materials to build bridges. Ask if anyone got any ideas for bridge building from bridges other couples identified.

Learning: Talk briefly about the importance of time together for communication and companionship. Share some of your own struggles balancing time and relationships even if you have not solved the problem. Being vulnerable will increase your effectiveness as a facilitator.

Ask couples to share in their groups what they discovered about time and priorities when they did Exercise E on page 36 in Chapter 2. To conclude, stress the importance of having our time controlled by our priorities rather than pressures.

Do a brief lecturette on differences in communication styles. Illustrate with your own differences and ask participants to share their differences. Emphasize that differences are learned and can be unlearned if one really wants to, but that differences can also be accommodated in a loving relationship.

Ask participants to list three issues about which they are likely to get defensive when approached by their spouse. Have them share these with their partner. Then ask them to individually write how they would like their partner to approach them in relation to each issue. Again, take turns sharing these.

Planning: Have each person select from the partner's list one issue s/he is willing to raise during the next week as the spouse has suggested. Have each agree to follow the requested behavior as closely as possible and try to control defensiveness. If your group meets weekly, ask couples to set a specific time during the week when they will read and do the exercises in Chapter 3.

Session 3: What to Say and How to Say It

Connecting: Ask couples to do Exercise F: Ten and Ten (Chapter 2, page 39). If time is limited, use five minutes to write feelings and five minutes to share with partner.

Assessing: Briefly review parts of the awareness wheel and ask for questions. Have couples share in their small group the part of the wheel they are most aware and the part they are least aware. Then have them discuss which parts they are most willing to share with their partners and which they are least willing to share.

Learning: Have each person do Exercise H: Developing Self-Awareness (Chapter 3, page 60). Ask them to use a different event than when they did the exercise at home.

List on newsprint the Rules for Self-Disclosure discussed in Chapter 3 (page 61). Describe each briefly. Have couples dialogue privately the events they worked on above using the self-disclosure skills.

Planning: Ask couples to identify a rule for self-disclosure each is willing to work on this week. If your group meets weekly, ask couples to set a specific time during the week when they will read and do the exercises in Chapter 4.

Session 4: Avoiding Misunderstanding

Connecting: In small groups have couples talk about how they used the awareness wheel and self-disclosure skills during the week.

Assessing: In the large group talk about listening skills. Ask the group to identify characteristics of a good listener and of a poor listener. List these on newsprint. Have couples assess their progress on "Evaluating Our Listening Skills" exercise (Chapter 4, page 78).

Learning: Briefly identify the three steps in paraphrasing. Have each person identify and send a message to his/her partner to be paraphrased. Briefly identify the points in giving positive and negative feedback. Ask each person to write, "How I would like my partner to give me positive feedback." Share with partner. Then write, "How I would like my partner to give me negative feedback," and share. Finally, have them tell their partners if there is any area in which they want no feedback. Review with the group Stuart's rules for feedback (page 85).

Planning: Have each person look back over Chapter 4 and select one skill s/he will work on during the week. If your group meets weekly, ask couples to set a specific time during the week when they will read and do the exercises in Chapter 5.

Session 5: Using Communication Skills to Resolve Conflict

Connecting: In small group have each person share his experiences with the skill s/he chose to practice last week. Ask each to decide if s/he wishes to choose a new skill or if s/he wants to continue on the same one. *Assessing:* Ask participants to stand up if they are "stuffers." Then ask "yellers" to stand. Have each person describe to his small group how conflict and anger were handled in the family in which s/he grew up. How does this affect the way s/he handles conflict and anger now?

Learning: Discuss the biblical material on anger stressing that anger is a natural emotion—that only the behavior that accompanies the anger can be judged good or bad. Describe the three-step process to handle anger. Ask couples to think back to a recent conflict. Have them discuss how the process could have helped them in that situation. Describe negotiation options. Ask couples to look at a conflict they have resolved and identify the type of negotiation they used. Do they use one type more than another?

Planning: Have couples agree on an issue and complete Exercise O: Resolving Conflict (Chapter 5, page 105). If your group meets weekly, have them set specific times during the week to do this and to read and do the exercises in Chapter 6.

Session 6: Using Communication Skills to Grow in Oneness

Connecting: Have couples use a large sheet of paper to draw a "Marriage Lifeline." Beginning with their wedding have them graph the "ups and downs" of their relationship. They may draw pictures or use words to identify events. Have each couple share its lifeline in the small group.

Assessing: Ask them to discuss as a couple what periods produced the most closeness. Were these at low or high points? How did that situation bring about closeness?

Learning: Discuss and list on newsprint, blocks to intimacy. Then discuss and list ways to build intimacy.

Planning: Ask each person to complete the following exercise. List three things "I want for me," three things "I want for you (my partner)," and three things "I want for us." Use the next six months as a time frame. Have couples privately discuss this exercise. Now have them look at the Growth Plan they completed at home (Chapter 6, page 118). Are the areas they identified in the above exercise included? Do they want to revise the plan in any way? Have couples share as much of their plans as they wish with their small group. Discuss the future of their contracts (Chapter 6, page 118).

Close the session with a prayer to rededicate these relationships and a petition for grace and guidance as they strive to honor the contracts made with each other.

THE CHURCH STUDY COURSE

The Church Study Course is a Southern Baptist educational system consisting of short courses for adults and youth combined with a credit and recognition system. More than five hundred courses are available in twenty-three subject areas. Credit is awarded for each course completed. These credits may be applied to one or more of over one hundred diploma plans in the recognition system. Diplomas are available for most leadership positions, and general diplomas are available for all Christians. These diplomas certify that a person has completed from five to eight prescribed courses.

Complete details about the Church Study Course system, courses available, and diplomas offered may be found in a current copy of *Church Study Course Catalog* and in the study course section of *Church Materials Catalog*. Study course materials are available from Baptist Book Stores.

The Church Study Course system is sponsored by the Sunday School Board, Woman's Missionary Union, and the Brotherhood Commission of the Southern Baptist Convention.

Requirements for Credit

The book is the text for course 17109 in the subject area The Christian Family. This course is designed for a minimum of five hours of group study. Credit may be earned in three ways.

1. *Group study.* Read the book and attend group sessions. If you are absent from one or more sessions, complete the learning exercises for the material missed.
2. *One-to-one study.* Read the book and complete the learning exercises with your spouse. Written work should be submitted to an appropriate church leader.
3. *Individual study.* Read the book and complete the learning exercises. Written work should be submitted to an appropriate church leader.

To Request Credit

A request for credit may be made on Form 725, Church Study Course Enrollment/Credit Request, and sent to the Awards Office, Baptist Sunday School Board, 127 Ninth Avenue North, Nashville, Tennessee 37234. The form on the following page may be used to request credit.

A record of your awards will be maintained by the Awards Office. Twice each year copies will be sent to churches for distribution to members.

CHURCH STUDY COURSE
ENROLLMENT/CREDIT REQUEST (FORM-725)

PERSONAL CSC NUMBER (If Known)

INSTRUCTIONS:
1. Please PRINT or TYPE.
2. COURSE CREDIT REQUEST—Requirements must be met. Use exact title.
3. ENROLLMENT IN DIPLOMA PLANS—Enter selected diploma title to enroll.
4. For additional information see the Church Study Course Catalog.
5. Duplicate additional forms as needed. Free forms are available from the Awards Office and State Conventions.

TYPE OR REQUEST: (Check all that apply)
- ☐ Course Credit
- ☐ Enrollment in Diploma Plan
- ☐ Address Change
- ☐ Name Change
- ☐ Church Change

DATE OF BIRTH → | Month | Day | Year

CHURCH

Church Name

Mailing Address

City, State, Zip Code

REQUEST FOR

- ☐ Mr.
- ☐ Mrs.
- ☐ Miss.

Name (First, Mi, Last)

Street, Route, or P.O. Box

City, State, Zip Code

COURSE CREDIT REQUEST

Course No.	Use Exact title
17109	1. *The Language of Married Love*
Course No.	Use Exact title
	2.
Course No.	Use Exact title
	3.
Course No.	Use Exact title
	4.
Course No.	Use Exact title
	5.

ENROLLMENT IN DIPLOMA PLANS

If you have not previously indicated a diploma(s) you wish to earn, or you are beginning to work on a new one(s), select and enter the diploma title from the current Church Study Course Catalog. Select one that relates to your leadership responsibility or interest. When all requirements have been met, the diploma will be automatically mailed to your church. No charge will be made for enrollment or diplomas.

→

Title of diploma	Age group or area
1.	
Title of diploma	Age group or area
2.	

Signature of Pastor, Teacher, or study Leader	Date

MAIL THIS REQUEST TO → CHURCH STUDY COURSE AWARDS OFFICE
RESEARCH SERVICES DEPARTMENT
127 NINTH AVENUE, NORTH
NASHVILLE, TENNESSEE 37234

FORM-725 (rev. 7-83)